I Look to You

Veronica Franklin

Dedication

To my mom, Nettie Lee Franklin, I will forever cherish and appreciate the love, sacrifice and dedication you gave to me and your family. I am so grateful, that God chose me to be one of your daughters. If I could be half the woman you were, I'd be great! I love you Mommy!

Acknowledgements

This book would not be possible without God, my family, church family and reading team: Trina, Jasmine, Tanzania, Sheryl, Davra, Davette and David. Thanks. Last, but definitely not least, my earthly hero, my Dad, David Franklin. Thank you for always loving, supporting and cheering me in all my endeavors. I love you and I'm so blessed to have you as a Dad and friend.

Table of Contents

Prologue (Damen)..p 6

Chapter 1 (Kimberly)..p 9

Chapter 2 (Damen)...p 14

Chapter 3 (Kimberly)..p 17

Chapter 4 (Damen)...p 25

Chapter 5 (Kimberly)..p 29

Chapter 6 (Josh)...p 47

Chapter 7 (Kimberly)... p 57

Chapter 8 (Josh)... p 61

Chapter 9 (Kimberly).. p 64

Chapter 10 (Josh)..p 68

Chapter 11 (Damen)... p 74

Chapter 12 (Kimberly)...p 77

Chapter 13 (Josh)..p 88

Chapter 14 (Kimberly).. p 95

Chapter 15 (Damen)... p 101

Chapter 16 (Josh).. p 107

Chapter 17 (Kimberly).. p 110

Chapter 18 (Josh).. p 115

Chapter 19 (Kimberly)... p 118

Chapter 20 (Josh)... p 125

Chapter 21 (Kimberly)... p 128

Chapter 22 (Damen).. p 135

Chapter 23 (Kimberly)... p 140

Chapter 24 (Josh)... p 144

Chapter 25 (Kimberly)... p 151

Chapter 26 (Josh)... p 158

Chapter 27 (Damen).. p 160

Prologue

Damen

1991

"No! No!" Damen rolled over as he heard screams. He immediately flung his bedroom door open. He saw his mother on the floor, his father standing over her, with a lock of her hair. His father lifted his right hand and punched her forcefully in the face.

"Stop it! Stop it!" Damen screamed as he pushed his dad with all of his might, causing his dad to slightly lose balance. His father quickly turned to Damen with a frown.

"Please Steve!" His mother pleaded as she slowly sat up. "Don't hurt . . ."

"Shut up woman! This jerk thinks he's a man!"

Damen had never raised his voice to his dad, yet alone put his hands on him. He was horrified. Damen lifted his head and shoulders. He was ready to receive whatever his dad was going to give, as long as it kept him off his mother.

"You little punk!" Steve exclaimed as he slapped Damen.

"Who do you think you are?"

Damen stood still as he looked his father dead in his eyes.

"Stop hitting my mom!"

"Who's gonna stop me?"

Damen swallowed hard.

"Meee . . . me."

His father laughed out loud and shook his head. He quickly grabbed Damen and shoved him into the wall. His mother ran towards Steve.

6

"Please Steve!" His mother intervened as she placed a hand on his chest. Steve looked at her as he let go of Damen.

"You better teach this jerk some manners, Karla, or I'll beat some sense into him!"

"I"ll take care of it. Damen let's get you back to bed." As Karla took Damen by the hand, she felt a pain so deep in the pit of her stomach. In the past, Steve had hit her, but never, had he put his hands on their children. Damen was only six years old. He shouldn't have to endure physical and emotional abuse. Karla looked at Damen who was looking up at her with tears in his eyes.

"I can't go to sleep Mommy. I won't!"

"Damen please! I will be okay. Your Dad has calmed down. He will fall asleep soon."
Karla tried to sound convincing as she cracked a faint smile.

Damen didn't seem to buy it.

"Damen, I need you to stay in your room and watch over Cam."

Cameron was his four year old sister. "I need you to protect her, not me." Karla continued with tears in her eyes.

"Mommy can take care of herself."

Damen looked at her and quickly agreed as he hugged her tightly. He hated to see his Mom cry and would agree to anything when he saw her crying.

They walked back into the bedroom. "Damen" Karla called.

"I love you my sweet boy."

"I love you too Mommy!"

Karla looked down at the bottom bunk and was relieved to see Cam, still sleeping.

Damen climbed up to the top bunk and laid on his back. He closed his eyes as his Mom kissed him on the forehead.

"Goodnight Damen." Karla slowly closed the door. Once the door was closed, Damen opened his eyes and looked up at the ceiling. He would not sleep; he had to think of a way to protect both Cam and his Mom.

Chapter 1

Kimberly

2015

Kimberly was beyond worried. She had called Damen several times at work and on his cell phone but to no avail. He had informed her that his Mom and Sister would be joining them for dinner. It was now, 7:45pm and no word from Damen, his Mom or Sister. Kimberly decided to call his mom.

"Hi Kimberly, how are you?"

"Hi Ms. Banks, have. . . "

"Karla." Karla interjected. She'd asked that Kim called her by her first name, Karla.

"Im sorry Karla, have you seen Damen?"

"Damen?"

"Yes, he was . . ."

"He's here having dinner with Cam and I, at the Grand Lux Cafe."

"Really?!" Kimberly responded.

She was infuriated. She had rushed home, prepared dinner for him and his family, only to have them go out to eat dinner without having the courtesy to call and inform her.

"Kimberly?"

"Yes."

"We were hoping to see you but Damen informed us that you had to work late tonight."

"Did he?" He had to be kidding her!

"Are you okay Kimberly?"

"I am Karla. . . I'm sorry; I was just worried about Damen. I totally forgot that he was having dinner with you and Cam tonight. Enjoy your dinner Karla."

"I will honey. Would you like to talk to Damen?"

"No, I just wanted to know that he was okay. Tell Cam I said hello."

"I will."

"Goodnight Karla."

"Good night Honey."

Kimberly hung up the phone, washed her hands and began to heat up some of the dinner she had prepared. She put away the rest of the food in disbelief. Kimberly didn't understand. She got along well with Damen's mom and sister, or at least she thought. Kimberly took her plate out of the microwave, sat down and began to eat.

Once she was finished eating, she walked towards the bathroom. She needed a relaxing bath to soothe her nerves. Kimberly filled the tub with soap and water. She placed several candles across the tub and lit them. After prepping, she slowly climbed into the tub. Kimberly closed her eyes and soaked.

Kimberly got out of the tub, applied lotion to her skin and placed on her nightgown as she climbed into bed. She looked at the clock, it now read, 10:07. Kimberly shook her head; some of Damen's actions were displeasing and questionable. Yet, she loved Damen with every ounce of her being. That's why she agreed to marry him but her intuition told her those problems needed to be addressed before they said, "I do."

Kimberly must have dozed off. When she awoke, Damen was standing on his side of the bed, taking off his shirt. He was a sight to see, physically fit, 6' 5, smooth caramel skin with a low fade, nicely trimmed beard with a small goatee. Kimberly looked at the clock, 11:05. Damen cracked her, his million dollar smile.

"Hey Doll, sorry to wake you."

"Sorry to wake me? Damen what happened this evening? I was worried sick! You didn't answer my calls, nor did you tell me that you were going to take your family out to eat."

"I know baby, my phone died. I got busy and I totally forgot that I asked you to prepare dinner for my family."

"How convenient"

Damen looked at Kimberly.

"What do you mean how convenient? Do you think I'm lying? Why would I have to lie to you? Hmmm? You're not my wife and you're starting to nag me like. . ."

"Not your wife, excuse me for thinking that I was going to be your wife!"

"Yeah poor Kim."

"Don't act like this is my fault. Do not turn things around and act as if it's my fault and that I'm overreacting."

"You are, you always do. I don't have time for this."

Damen walked into the master's bathroom and began brushing his teeth. Kimberly turned from his direction. She knew her actions were justified. She was not overreacting. How could he come home and act as if everything was fine? Kimberly could not believe him! Kimberly heard a vibrating sound on the night stand. She looked on the stand and found Damen's phone, not dead but vibrating. Kimberly lifted the phone and it read, "Tony." Before Kimberly could say a word Damen snatched the phone from her hand.

"Why are you checking my phone? I told you it died. I need to charge it!"

"Liar!"

"I'm not lying!"

"You are being a jerk."

"What did you say to me?"

"Liar! You are being a jerk!"

Damen slapped Kimberly right across the face.

Kimberly was stunned. Damen had never hit her before!

Kimberly jumped out of the bed with tears in her eyes. She was in more pain

emotionally than physically. Kimberly walked towards the door. Damen blocked it.

"Damen move!"

"Baby please! . . . I am so sorry." Damen pleaded as he took her by the arm.

"Don't touch me!" Kimberly yelled as she tried to pull away from him.

He pulled her closer to him and held her in his arms as Kimberly tried to push away

from him.

"Please Kim."

Kimberly began to sob as he held her.

"Please forgive me."

Kimberly was silent.

"I promise Doll, I will never hit you again. I love you."

Damen looked down at Kimberly as she looked at him in disbelief.

"Damen get out, Get out!"

"Okay, okay. I'll sleep in the guestroom and give you some time alone. Come here; let

me see if you're okay. Did I bruise you?"

Damen walked closer to her, turned her face to the side he'd slapped and kissed her

there.

"I'm so sorry."

Kimberly wondered was Damen really sorry or was he trying to manipulate her into

staying?

Damen looked at her with puppy dog eyes and lowered his voice.

"I love you Doll. I totally lost my cool.

I know this is no excuse but I am under a lot of pressure at work and it will never

happen again. I promise."

"Damen. . ." Kimberly started her voice shaky and raspy. "I love you too." Kimberly

continued as she looked Damen straight in the eyes.

"But if you ever hit me again, I will leave you and never look back. Do you hear me?"

Damen nodded. "I hear you loud and clear."

He walked over, held her face with his hands and kissed her. He continued to kiss her

as he eased down the strap to her nightgown.

"Goodnight Damen."

Damen gave her a slight smile.

"Goodnight Doll, I'll see you in the morning."

Kimberly started to walk back towards the bed.

"Hey Doll!"

Kimberly turned around.

Damen mouthed, "I love you."

Kimberly smiled and mouthed, "I love you too."

Chapter 2

Damen

Damen closed the bedroom door and walked towards the guest bedroom. Once in the guestroom, Damen crawled into bed as he looked up at the ceiling. He really did love Kimberly. He never hit a woman, nor had he ever wanted to. Damen lost his cool, the minute he heard the word jerk. As a kid, his dad referred to him as jerk and punk so much that he started to respond to it. When he heard Kimberly, use the word he flashed back. Was he turning into his Dad?

He wondered. Damen loved Kimberly and he wanted to spend the rest of his life with her. I am nothing like my Dad. I lost my temper. He knew he would never hit Kimberly again. Damen closed his eyes. *I've got to make it up to her.* He thought as he turned on his side.

* * * *

Damen rolled over; he immediately got up and went into the kitchen. He washed his hands, grabbed a couple of eggs, cracked them and began to stir. Once he was finished he put bread in the toaster and placed bacon into the skillet. He started the coffee pot. Flowers would have been nice but he would make do with what he had.

His phone vibrated in his pocket.

"Hi Toya."

"Hello Sexy, I called you last night. What happened?"

"It was a chaotic night."

"Really, will you tell me about it tonight?"

"Uhh . . . negative, I need to smooth things over with my girl. Like I said it was a chaotic night."

"Ah! Damen you promised."

"I know but I can't. I gotta go. I will call you later."

Damen hung up the phone.

He walked over to the bedroom. Kimberly was lying on the bed still asleep. She was beautiful. Kimberly had a petite curvy body, flawless dark skin, big dimples and shoulder length hair that splayed over the pillow. Damen smiled as he closed the door.

He went back into the kitchen to tend to the food. He prepared her plate and placed it on the portable tray. Damen walked into the bedroom as Kimberly rolled over.

"Something smells good." Kimberly said with a smile.

"Lucky for you, it's just as good as it smells." Damen replied as he kissed her. He took the fork and grabbed some eggs and placed it up to Kimberly's mouth.

"Impressive." Kimberly said with a smile.

"I knew you would like it."

Damen looked at her intently.

Kimberly frowned. "What's wrong?"

"I'm sorry for putting my hands on you. I was totally wrong for doing that."

Kimberly bit her bottom lip and nodded her head as she looked down.

Damen lifted her head by gently lifting her chin.

"I want you to forgive me, I need you to. I know it may take some time but I will work to gain your trust."

Kimberly looked at Damen.

"I am going to forgive you Damen, I love you but I need some time."

"I love you too and I'll give you all the time you need."

"Thanks for understanding."

Ding Dong.

Kimberly and Damen looked at each other with bemusement.

Damen walked to the door and opened it.

"Hi Damen! How are you?"

"I'm good Dee." She was really the last person Damen wanted to see. Dee was short for

Nadine. She was Kimberly's nosey, very opinionated little Sister.

Dee walked into the house.

"Something smells good! What ya'll cooking in here?"

"Breakfast" Damen responded.

"Where's my Sister?" Nadine asked as she walked through the house.

Chapter 3

Kimberly

"Hi Dee" Kimberly walked towards her and gave her a hug. Dee was Nadine's nickname.

"What a pleasant surprise."

"I'm glad you said that girl."

Kimberly laughed. "What are you talking about Dee? It's always nice to see you."

Damen looked at Nadine and Kimberly.

"I'll let you ladies talk." Damen walked into the bedroom and closed the door.

"What's going on Dee?" Kimberly asked.

"Well Kim . . . I kinda need a place to stay."

"Okay, you know you can stay here, I'll talk to Damen. . . is everything okay?"

"Yes and no."

"What's going on?"

"I quit my job a few months ago, so I lost my place. My boss . . . girl! She was working my nerves. I told her a piece of my mind and where she could go then I walked out the door."

"I thought you loved that job?"

"I did, but not the boss. Honey she was a piece of work. And you know me, I don't take keenly to rude people. Are you sure Damen's gonna be cool with this?

"Yes."

"I mean you're sweet and all but Damen's a firecracker. I 'm not sure how long I'll need to stay with you. I am looking and will continue to look for a job but I can't give you a time frame"

"I'll talk to him Dee."

"Please, cause I don't want to go to Grandma's. You know how she is with, Jesus this and Jesus that. Girl I would go insane!"

Kimberly laughed. "Granny loves sharing the gospel but she's not that bad."

"Yeah, you weren't singing that tune when you told her you were moving in with Damen."

"You're right, that's something I remember oh too well."

When Kimberly told her granny that she was moving in with Damen, her Grandmother went ballistics. She told her that she was going to hell and that no Granddaughter of hers should be shacking up. She continued to say that she raised her better than that, as she quoted biblical scriptures on marriage and fornication.

Her Grandmother constantly pointed out how God honors marriage. Kimberly remembered leaving the house in tears.

"Kim?! Are you listening to me girl?"

"I'm sorry Dee. What did you say?"

"I asked you when you were going to talk to Damen? I am at a hotel right now. I can stay there for about 2-3 days but that's about it."

"I will talk to Damen today. It will be okay."

Just then Damen walked out of the bedroom, showered and fully dressed.

Breathtaking Kimberly thought. They'd been together for two years and he still gave her butterflies, even after last night.

"You'll talk to me about what Doll?"

"It's a long story, I will tell you about it a little later." Kimberly knew Damen and he didn't bite his tongue. Her sister needed a place to stay and she didn't want him to say something that might hurt her feelings. They would have this conversation when Dee left the house.

"Alright then, I have to run out for a bit. I should be back in about an hour or so." He kissed Kimberly before giving Dee a quick nod.

"Good seeing you again Dee. Maybe we could double date sometimes."

"It's good seeing you too but I'm no longer with Paul. We broke up about two months ago."

"Why doesn't that surprise me?" Damen replied as he shook his head.

"I don't know. Why don't you tell me?" Dee replied as she looked at Kimberly.

"Dee that's something internal, only you can answer that. Take care of yourself." Damen looked at Kimberly "I love you doll."

"I love you too Babe." Kimberly responded.

Damen closed the door as Dee shook her head and looked at Kimberly. Kimberly smiled.

"Hey, Dee, I can talk to my supervisor about getting you a job at the desk."

"Kim, I appreciate that, but with my temper? I am not trying to mess up your place of employment because of my mouth and temper. I got some money in my savings. I should be okay. I can give you and Damen about $250 a month. I hope that's okay?"

"Dee you're my sister. Stop that, you're not going to pay us."

"Sister Girl, love does not pay your bills or feed your stomach. $250 or no deal."

Kimberly stared silently at Dee.

"Come on girl, you know I don't have anywhere else to go. Take my money!"

"I would rather you save that money until you get back on your feet."

"Kim, I'm no scrub, if I'm gonna stay here, I'm going to pay you and Damen."

"You are so persistent."

"So it's a deal?"

"Deal Sis."

"Great, I hope Damen's cool with this.

I am going to go to the bank and then grab a few things from the hotel. I'm going to have lunch with a friend and I'll call you."

"No." Kimberly interjected. "I'll call you after I've talked to Damen."

"Alright Sis, I love you."

"I love you too Sis."

Kimberly walked with Dee to the front door. She watched her sister as she got into her car and drove off. Kimberly closed the door. She quickly told herself that everything would be okay. She would talk to Damen and Dee would stay with them unto she got back on her feet. Kimberly wanted to believe that but she knew Damen would not be fond of the idea.

Kimberly grabbed her breakfast, warmed it and picked up her bible. She started reading John 15:16,
Ye have not chosen me, but I have chosen you, and ordained you, that ye should go and bring forth fruit, and that your fruit should remain: that whatsoever ye shall ask of the Father in my name, he may give it you. Kimberly closed her eyes and prayed. God help me bring forth fruit according to your will so that whatsoever, I asked in Jesus name you may give it to me as you see fit. Help me grow in you. Amen.

Kimberly began to clean the house. She played music as she began to sort the laundry by colors. She didn't even hear Damen come in. He walked up behind her, placed his arms around her waist and gently kissed her on the neck. Kimberly smiled. "We need to talk."

"I don't like conversations that begin with. . ." Damen made quotation marks with his hands as he continued, "We need to talk."

Kimberly turned around to face him. She looked at Damen. He had a slight frown. "Damen I . . . "

"Wait I have something for you." He left the bedroom, and returned with a vase filled with two dozens of white and red roses. Kimberly's favorite.

"Damen!" Kimberly exclaimed with a smile.

Damen smiled and handed her the vase with roses.

He held up his index finger and left the room. Kimberly smiled as she looked at the roses and shook her head.

When Damen returned he held a large bag. Kimberly looked at Damen with bewilderment. He took the roses and placed them on the nightstand.

"Here." Damen held the bag out towards Kimberly.

Kimberly looked at Damen.

"It's not going to bite you I promise."

Kimberly sat on the bed as she opened the bag.

"Damen, really?!" Damen had purchased a Michael Kors hand bag with the matching wallet.

This was him trying to apologize for last night. Kimberly wanted him to apologize with his actions not with material things.

"Damen you can't buy my forgiveness. You know I am not materialistic."

"Kimberly, I just purchased the gifts as a token of my love and appreciation. I would never try to buy your forgiveness because it's priceless. You're worth more than I could ever afford, truthfully."

God I love this man. Kimberly thought as she walked up to Damen and kissed him. She hugged him tightly.

"I love you Damen."

"I love you too Doll."

Kimberly smiled.

"There's one more little gift inside the bag." Kimberly looked up at Damen and walked back to the bag and lifted the tissue paper from the bag. She saw a small red Cartier box. Kimberly opened the box and it was a beautiful diamond bracelet.

"Thank you."

"I take it, you like?"

"Yes I do. Thanks Babe"

"You're welcome and since we are showing our love."

Damen kissed her.

"And appreciation." He continued as he moved her hair to the side and kissed her neck.

"Damen we need to talk."

"We can talk, I'm listening." He continued kissing her.

"Seriously Damen?"

Damen stopped and looked at Kimberly.

"Is this about last night?" Damen asked while looking puzzled.

"No, this is about Dee."

"Dee?"

"Yes, she needs a place to stay and . . ."

"She wants to stay here and you told her yeah. Right?" Damen interjected.

"I did, so you understand?"

"I didn't say I understood. She takes advantage of you."

"How? We have a place to stay and she needs a place to stay. You would do the same for Cam."

"I would, but Cam is not calling me two times a month for money that she never pays back, nor is she calling me to bail her out of jail for fighting not to mention her quitting jobs just because she feels like it. And my favorite, asking you to cosign a car for her only to ask you to make the last four payments. I don't like that."

"She's my sister!"

"I know. That's why I haven't intervened. I don't like anyone taking advantage of you and that's what she does. "Damen shook his head. "How long is she staying?"

"She doesn't know."

"Oh no! I can't do it!" Damen shook his head.

"Damen, she is no longer working but she's searching for a job. Dee will have something soon."

Damen lifted his eyebrow.

"Damen . . . she'll find something soon."

"I hope so."

"So you agree to let her stay with us until she gets on her feet?"

"I don't, but you already told her yes." Damen stared at Kimberly.

Plus, I owe you, so I won't say no. But! . . . Now you owe me."

He grabbed Kimberly as she laughed out loud. She was glad he agreed.

Chapter 4

Damen

Damen smiled as he looked over at Kimberly who was asleep. *We needed this reconnecting*. Damen thought. He always called love making reconnecting. He looked on the nightstand and grabbed his phone and took it into the bathroom with him as he closed the door. He dialed Toya's number.

"Hi Sexy."

"Hi Toya."

"Are you on your way over?"

"No, I'm not coming over. We need to end our friends with benefits arrangement."

"Why because now your little virgin's putting out?"

"Yes and no."

He and Toya had started their friends with benefits arrangement a year after he and Kimberly started dating. Damen knew it wasn't right. Toya had a crush on him for years. Once Kimberly told him that she was a virgin and wanted to wait till marriage Damen told himself he'd wait a year and if he couldn't persuade her, he would definitely find someone else. However, Damen fell for Kimberly. After a year passed, he didn't want to let her go. Yet he told himself he had needs so he talked to Toya and the rest became history.

"Toya, I told you upfront what kind of arrangement this was. Don't play the victim."

"I am not playing the victim! I just ask you a questioned."

"And I answered it." Damen responded sternly.

"Okay, so you are ending our friends with benefits relationship?"

"Our arrangement, yes."

"What Damen wants he gets, right?"

Damen was silent.

"What Damen speechless?"

"What else would you like me to say? Let's stay in touch? Come on, I don't owe you anything."

"You don't. Forgive me for thinking that maybe I meant something to you."

"Forgiven"

The last thing Damen wanted was for Toya to feel sorry for herself. He was direct in letting her know upfront the arrangements. He never promised her anything but a good time.

"So, I guess I will see you around work."

"Yeap. Take care of yourself Toya."

"Yeah you do the same Damen.

Kimberly's a lucky girl."

"I think we're both lucky. Gotta go."

"Yeah, I don't want to keep you from her. That is where you are now right?"

"Don't go stalker, psycho on me Toya."

Toya laughed. "Yeah you don't have to worry, I'm not a stalker or psycho, just a little hurt but I'll get over it."

"Great, I gotta go."

Damen hung up the phone. *She took that as if we were in a relationship*, he thought. He got involved with her because she was not the clingy; I need to be with you every minute type of girl. Why was she acting brand new? Damen shook his head. He had a lot to think about and Toya was not one of them. He flushed the toilet and ran the water across his hands as he opened the door.

Kimberly was still asleep. Damen climbed back into bed and turned the television on. He was going to be a good and faithful man. Kimberly deserved a man that would treat her right. She had given a lot for their relationship. He knew she loved him with all of her heart. He hoped she knew just how much he loved her. He still couldn't shake the look she'd given him when he slapped her. They had to put this behind them. That was the past. He was looking forward to the two of them building their relationship with new memories but now they had to share their home with Dee. She was nosey, loud and opinionated. He hoped her stay would be short, very short. Damen looked down as Kimberly began to roll over next to him. She opened her eyes.

"Hi Doll, did you sleep well?"

"Very." Kimberly said with a smile.

"What time is it?"

"1:15, why?"

"Because I have a hot date with this very smart, attractive, fun and outgoing man."

"Oh really?"

"Yes."

"He sounds like trouble."

"He is . . . "

"Oh really?" Damen asked as he laughed out loud.

27

Kimberly laughed and climbed out of bed.

"Let me get lunch started. Are you hungry?"

"Starving."

"Okay, let me prepare something. I'll be back."

"No rush, I don't want to keep you from your hot date."

Kimberly laughed as she walked out of the bedroom.

Damen began to flip through several channels. He stopped the television on basketball the Bulls against the Cavaliers.

Ring! Ring! Damen looked at Kimberly's phone and it read, "Dee."

"Hi Dee."

"Damen? What are you doing answering my sister's phone? Does she answer your phone?"

"Be quiet Dee; hold on while I get Kim."

Damen got up out of the bed and walked into the kitchen where Kimberly was preparing sandwiches. She was cutting the tomatoes. Kimberly looked up at Damen who was extending the phone towards her.

"It's Dee."

Kimberly wiped her hands off with the dish towel and took the phone.

"Thanks Damen."

Damen lifted his eyebrows. "Yeah."

He walked back into the bedroom. He could not wait until this was over.

Chapter 5

Kimberly

"Hi Dee."

"Hey girl. Why is he answering your phone?"

"I don't mind, I don't have anything to hide."

"I know you don't but you should have limits and boundaries. I know you're not going around answering Damen's phone, because he ain't going for that."

Kimberly shook her head.

"Dee we trust each other."

"Kim sometimes your trust, borderlines being naive."

"So now I'm naive?"

"Kim you tend to . . . how can I say this, overlook people's flaws when you love and care for them. You love unconditionally but love has limits."

"Yeah so I've heard."

"Kim don't get all sentimental on me."

"I am not getting sentimental."

"Yes you are but I still love you."

"I love you too Dee."

"Did you talk to Damen about me staying with ya'll?"

"I have and he has agreed."

"What!? Did you tell him everything?"

"I told him everything, he agreed."

"You told him that my stay would be indefinitely?"

"Yes, I did."

"Wow girl what kind of persuading did you have to do?"

"Not a lot, Damen's pretty reasonable."

"Well that's good to know."

"I can come over and help you with your bags. I will see if Damen and a couple of his friends can help with moving your furniture into storage."

"Girl I already sold my furniture. All I have are my clothes and jewelry."

"Really? Will everything fit in your car?"

"Kim I need your help."

"Okay, I'll be there.

"Thanks again Kim. I really do appreciate it."

"I'll come and help you with your things around 3:00, if that works for you?"

"That's works fine."

"Good so 3:00 it is."

"See you at 3:00 Kim."

"Bye Dee, see you then."

Kimberly ended the call and sat it on the counter as she washed her hands and continued preparing their lunch.

Once she was finished with their sandwiches, she sliced the sandwiches diagonally and placed carrots and grapes on the plates. She grabbed the bottled waters and placed one on the counter as she grabbed a tray and sat Damen's plate and water on it. Kimberly walked into the bedroom and handed him the tray.

"Here you go Babe."

"Thanks." Damen took the tray.

"Dee's really grateful you agreed to let her stay here with us."

"She should be." Damen replied as he took a bite from his sandwich.

"She appreciates it and so do I."

"I only did it for you. I hope she doesn't make me regret it."

"She won't, thanks Damen."

"The things we do for love."

Kimberly smiled as she went to the kitchen and grabbed her lunch and took it in the bedroom. She climbed back in bed with Damen and began to watch the game with him until 2:45.

"Damen, I am going over to the hotel where Dee's staying. I am going to help her move things."

"What?!"

"She only has a few clothes and some jewelry. She's sold all of her furniture so it should be pretty easy."

"Hmmm. . . call me if you need any help."

"I will." Kimberly kissed Damen. "I love you."

"I love you too." Damen gave a slight smile.

Kimberly waved and got in her car.

When she arrived, Dee met her at the door.

"Girl I really appreciate this. Here is the $250."

"I told you not to worry about it."

"And I told you I'm no scrub." She took Kimberly's hand and placed the money in her hand.

"I'm not taking no for an answer."

Kimberly shook her head. She was going to put the money away and save it for her when she moved. Kimberly would give her the money to help furniture her new place or

31

to buy electronics, etc. Kimberly walked over to the closet. "I can place some of your suitcases in my car. How many do you have?"

"I only have three they'll all fit in your car. I sold the car for $1500."

"What?!"

"Yeah Kim. I can use all the money I can get."

"That's exactly why you shouldn't give me any money." Kimberly tried to place the money back into Dee's hand but Dee made a fist with both of her hands and shook her head.

"I'm not taking the money Kim, it's yours. You can't stay anywhere for free."

"Yes, you can. I'm family!"

"Kim you're not winning this one. I'm going to pay you and Damen for staying with you. I know it's not much but . . . "

"It's enough Dee."

"So it's a deal?"

"Negotiable."

Dee and Kimberly smiled before loading her things in the car. Dee checked out of the hotel and they headed to Kimberly's condo. Damen met them at the door. He walked to the trunk of the car and grabbed two of the large suitcases. Dee grabbed the other suitcase as Kimberly closed the trunk.

Dee headed into the door and Kimberly followed behind her. Kimberly looked up towards the sky *Lord I pray that you fill our home with love, peace and joy. Guide us in Jesus name. Amen.*

Kimberly closed the door.

Damen had placed Dee's bags into the guest room. Dee walked into the guestroom and sat her bag down.

"Thanks again you two. I appreciate it."

"You're welcome." Kimberly responded.

Damen gave a slight smile as he walked out and into the master bedroom.

Dee looked at Kimberly.

Kimberly smiled at Dee.

"Get comfortable. Make yourself at home."

"I will, thanks Sis." Dee sat down on the bed."

"If you need anything, just let me know."

"Thanks. Can you close the door, while I settle in my room?" Dee asked.

"Sure." Kimberly closed the door and walked into the master bedroom.

"Ring! Ring!" Kimberly looked down at her phone.

"Toya Marks" Kimberly frowned.

"Hello? This is Kimberly. Who? Toya?"

"How did you get my number? Damen? Damen gave you my number?" Kimberly looked at Damen.

Damen gave a slight smile and beckoned for the phone. Kimberly was curious.

"Why are you calling?"

Damen quickly grabbed the phone.

"Remember, I said contact her for emergency purposes only."

"Yeah, I understand. My number's still the change. I will update all of that information on Monday. Thanks Toya." Damen hung up the phone. He shook his head and gave Kimberly a smile.

"That couldn't wait until Monday?"

Kimberly looked at Damen seriously.

"She's very dedicated."

Damen shrugged. "I guess."

"Is she dedicated to the job or you?"

"What is that suppose to mean?"

"It means I don't buy it. Are you cheating on me?"

"Kimberly that's foolish. You know I'm not cheating."

"Do I? I want to believe you but . . ."

"What's stopping you from believing me?"

"Your demeanor, your actions, the minute I mentioned Toya, you were on edge."

"Sure, I'm cheating on you and I gave her your number so the two of you could compare notes over coffee. Kimberly please! I'm outta here. I really don't have time for this."

Kimberly watched as Damen stormed out of the house and slammed the door.

"Dee quickly opened her bedroom door."

"Girl! What's going on?"

"It's okay, Damen and I got into a disagreement."

"Over what? . . . Me?"

"No, Dee."

"I don't want to cause problems. Man! This has got to be a record for me."

"Dee, Sis I'm serious. This had nothing to do with you. It was about his job."

"His job girl? Did he get fired? How does a lawyer get fired?"

"He didn't get fired."

"Then what?"

"He's been taking work home with him." *Literally* Kimberly thought.

"I told you Damen was a thrill seeker. The type of guy that gets bored easily, an adventure junkie. He's too much for you. And if you marry him, you will spend the rest of your life chasing him and his thrills."

Kimberly was not in the mood to hear reasons as to why Damen might cheat on her or why their relationship would not work.

"Dee this is not the time to tell me you think Damen is not right for me. Yes, Damen and I are different. But I love him. He's smart kind, outgoing and adventurous."

"Then when? I told you in the beginning of your relationship, heck, even before. He's a ladies man. I stopped bugging you about him because I told myself that he made you happy."

"He does."

"You can't fool me. You've been acting as if you've got a lot on your mind and I know it's him. You usually tell Grandma and I everything. So when you talking in code, giving brief responses it's something he's done or doing?"

"That's not true."

"Yes it is. Let me guess you're ready to set a wedding date and Damen is not ready."

"What?! No Damen wants to get married and start a family. We have not set a wedding date yet, but we haven't fought over setting a wedding date."

"Look I'm not trying to upset you any more than you are but I know how much you want to marry him so that you can obey The Word."

"We can change the subject."

"Kim if Damen really makes you happy, I'm all for it. You're my big sister and I love you. I want you to be happy."

Kimberly looked Dee in the eyes.

"I am happy. I love Damen. He makes me happy. Yes, we have our ups and downs but I'm totally in love with him."

Dee smiled.

"Okay, good. Should we watch a chick flick?"

"Sounds good but maybe later Dee."

"Okay Sis."

Kimberly walked into her bedroom and closed the door.

God I know I have not been praying the way I should or even reading the bible like I use to. Have mercy on my family and I. Strengthen, lead and guide me in all aspects of my life. In Jesus name I pray Amen.

"Knock, Knock.

"Come in."

"Hi baby."

"Grandma!"

"Don't act so surprise."

Kimberly hugged her Grandma. *Okay what's going on?* Kimberly thought. *Granny has that concern look on her face.*

"Is everything okay Granny?"

"I don't know I'm a little concern."

"Concerned . . . about what?"

"You, Kimme."

"Me. . . . but why?"

"Dee called me and told me that you and Damen were having problems and that he doesn't want to set a wedding date."

"That's not true. I already told Dee that we didn't have a fight over setting a wedding date. Why would she call you after I told her no?"

"Perhaps she doesn't believe you."

"She should, I have no reason to lie."

"Hmmm?" Kimberly's Grandmother looked her up and down with her hands on her hip.

"Chile I tell you." She shook her head.

"What's wrong Granny?"

"I don't like this idea of you and Damen shacking up. That's why the two of you are having problems, especially with setting a wedding date. He has you here in this condo, living with and catering to his needs. It's just not right. I did not raise you like this. If he loves you the way he claims and the way that you say he does, he would make an honest woman out of you and marry you."

"Granny we are getting married."

"Yes, the two of you are doing things backwards. God honors marriage. The bible says,

"Who so findeth a wife, findeth a good thing, and obtaineth favour of the Lord."

Kimberly nodded her head, "Yes Ma'am"

"Don't yes Ma'am me, listen Kimme . . . "

"Granny we've had this conversation before. You know I love and respect your opinions but I love Damen. We are going to get married and the Lord will honor our marriage."

"Kimmie, I don't understand. I never had problems out of you. You always got good grades and stayed out of trouble all your years of school, high school and college. You were going to church on Tuesdays and Sundays faithfully you . . . "

"Granny I still go to church on Sundays."

"Every Sunday?"

"Not every Sunday Granny but you see me there at least two Sundays a month. You know my work schedule. . . "

"But what about bible study on Tuesdays? I can't remember, the last time I saw you at bible study."

"It's been a while."

"I know Damen is a charmer but lure him in, don't allow him to lure you further into the world. I told you not to get a man that did not put God first. You need a Christian man, someone to help you grow spiritually. You do not want to be unequally yoked. You know what the bible says. . . "

"Granny, I am familiar with that verse." Kimberly responded.

"Then live by it baby. Live by it."

Growing up Kimberly's Grandmother instilled religion in them with a subtle approach. She said she wanted to live a life that reflected her beliefs in hopes of her Granddaughters following her by living Godly lives. Lately she had been very blatant and judgmental that was out of character for her. *Was it because of her and Damen?* Kimberly thought.

Kimberly met Damen her senior year of college. She had only dated one guy before him, Joshua. He was her high school sweetheart but he ended their relationship abruptly when he left for the services. Like her Grandmother had stated Damen was a charmer and she fell for him hard. He was kind, smart, outgoing and downright gorgeous.

Once Damen found out that Kimberly was a Christian and was saving herself for marriage he was understanding and respectful. Damen started attending church services and later joined her church. Kimberly thought he was perfect. She slowly found herself missing bible studies for date nights with him. Their kisses went from pecks to more passionate kisses. Damen encouraged and she allowed a little more and more. Kimberly reminded Damen about her beliefs and marriage. A month later he'd proposed. She was on cloud nine. One kiss lead to more than she'd planned. Though disappointed that she didn't wait for marriage Kimberly fell in love with him even more. Now six months later, Kimberly still faced the consequences. She had called and told her Grandmother what transpired. She still held resentment towards both her and Damen.

"Kimberly, are you listening to me?" Her Grandmother asked firmly.

"Granny Damen and I are still getting married. I'm sorry you had to come over here under false pretenses, but as always, I am happy to see you."

"I'm happy to see you as well but I know something's going on with you I raised you, so I know when something's bothering you. When you are ready to talk, I am here for you."

"I'm fine Granny, really. I am going to hurt Dee. She had you worrying for nothing."

"Don't hurt her, she's just concern, we're concern. We want the best for you."

"I know."

Dee walked into the bedroom.

"Is it safe to come in?"

"For now" Kimberly responded.

"Not so much when Granny leaves."

"Did you hear that Granny?" Dee said with a smile.

"I did, let's hope she changes her mind."

Dee smiled and looked at Kimberly who was looking at her.

"I doubt it."

"So Dee what's been going on with you?"

"Yes, I mean you've done a really good job of telling her about me and you're suspicions. Tell Granny about you."

Dee rolled her eyes as their Grandmother continued.

"Yes, Dee. Kimmie calls me often, checking on me and informing me on what's going on with her. You on the other hand, will call me occasionally after I've called you several times."

"Yeah, because Kim tells you everything and will answer all your questions regarding me."

"It's not the same. Plus, Kimmie's very selective with the information she shares with me concerning you."

"I see" Dee said with a nod.

"But there's not much going on with me. I'm happy, healthy and looking for a new job. I have a few prospective opportunities that look promising."

"So you're looking for another job? I thought you loved your job."

"I did but my boss was starting to work my nerves."

"Be patient, something will work out."

"I hope so Granny." Dee responded while shaking her head.

The ladies walked into the living room and sat on the sofa.

Kimberly went into the kitchen. She grabbed a bag of pretzels and placed some into a bowl, before she grabbed some bottled water. Kimberly sat the bowl of pretzels on the table and handed her Grandmother and Dee some water.

"Thank you baby."

"You're welcome Granny. Can I offer you anything else? Food, tea?"

"No Kimmie, I'm fine, have a seat and sit with us."

Kimberly smiled and walked over and sat on the sofa.

"Joshua's coming back to town."

"What!" Dee exclaimed "When?"

"I'm not really sure but I know it will be soon."

Kimberly looked at her Grandmother.

"Ooh this should be interesting Kim!" Dee said with a big smile.

"How so?"

"Your first love is coming back to town."

"I'm in love with Damen. I wish Josh nothing but the best but he and I are the past."

"That may be true but he's going through a lot and he needs friends and family."

Kimberly's Grandmother added. She continued. "He lost his wife two years ago. He and his two children are coming here to help his mom with his dad."

"What happened to Mr. Crawley?"

"He's going to have surgery to remove tumors as a precautionary measure."

"Oh wow! Kimberly exclaimed.

"Yeah and Josh wants to support his mom and dad."

"That's understanding, wow!" Dee said shaking her head.

"That's the way Josh is, very unselfish and dedicated. I always liked Joshua."

"Yes Granny, you always loved Josh." Kimberly replied.

"Yes, Josh came to me. He told me that he didn't want to hurt you. However, he couldn't promise he'd be back or how he would return. He thought it would be easier if he broke it off with you."

Kimberly stared at her Grandmother for a second. She never knew that.

"I didn't know that Granny. He told you but never me."

"Awww!" Dee said as she held her heart.

"He is the type of man; I always thought you'd marry Kimmie." Dee said as she nodded her head.

"I think that if you two gave Damen a chance, you'd like him really."

"Sweetie, I like him. I just don't like him for you. But at the end of the day I trust your opinion. You've never given me a reason to doubt you." Sadie stated.

Kimberly smiled and gave her Grandmother a hug.

The door opened and Damen walked in.

"Wow!" Damen said with a smile.

"Hello Damen."

"Hello. How are you Ms. Sadie?"

"I'm good." Sadie replied.

"So. . . have you been treating my Kimmie right ?"

"Absolutely! She means the world to me. All I want to do is make her happy."

"She wants to marry you."

"I know, I want to marry her too Ms. Sadie."

"It takes more than love to make a marriage work."

"Yes it does." Damen nodded his head.

"It takes dedication, compromise and unselfishness."

"Ms. Sadie, I'm dedicated to Kim. I love her."

"What do you love about her?"

Kimberly looked at Damen curious to hear his response on what he loved most about her.

"Everything."

"Be more specific Damen."

"I love that she's beautiful and kind."

"Anything else?"

"Yes, so many other things, like she's caring, giving and genuine."

Dee laughed out loud.

Damen looked over at Dee and back at Sadie. "Ms. Sadie, I love Kim. I'm going to spend the rest of my life making her happy."

"That's what I want for my girls. I want them to live, lives that are pleasing to God. I want them with God fearing husbands that will treat them with love and respect."

"See Ms. Sadie, we want some of the same things for Kim." Damen added.

"It's getting late Dee we better leave."

"Yes Grandma."

"Where's your car? I don't remember seeing it outside."

"It's in the shop, I will have it soon but I'm gonna stay here a bit longer."

"Okay Honey."

A"Granny, how did you get here? Kimberly asked.

"I caught a cab. I had to come over after I talked to Dee."

"Again, Granny, I'm sorry Dee had you come over under false pretenses. However, I did enjoy spending time with you." Kimberly said with a smile.

"I can take you home."

"Oh thanks Sweetie."

"Not a problem."

"Okay, well I'll see you later Dee." Sadie said as she gave Dee a hug.

"See you later Grandma. I love you."

"Love you too Honey."

"Damen it's been nice seeing you again."

"Same here Ms. Sadie. Take care of yourself."

Damen gave her a hug and helped her with her small sweater and handed her, her purse.

"Thank you."

"No worries Ms. Sadie."

Kimberly and Ms. Sadie got in Kimberly's car and drove off.

Once at her Sadie's house, Kimberly got out of the car and opened the door for her Grandmother.

"Kimberly!"

Kimberly turned around.

"Hello Mrs. Crawley."

"So nice to see you Kim."

"Nice seeing you as well."

"If it's not too much to ask, I was wondering if you could come and work with my husband for about two days a week on your off days? We will pay you of course. The doctors recommended that my husband have a nurse come by once or twice a week for about a month after James surgery."

"Ummm. . . when would you need me to start?"

"In about two weeks."

"Okay that should be . . . "

"Josh is coming back,so he will be at the house sometimes."

"That's fine." Kimberly responded.

"Great, I just wanted to give you the heads up. I know the two of you didn't end on the best of terms after he left for the services."

"Yes Mrs. Crawley, but that was so long ago. I've forgiven him."

"Oh great, he needs people his age he can talk to, people who want the best for him." Kimberly smiled.

"Hey chile how you doing?" Sadie asked

"I'm good Sadie. I was just asking Kimberly if she could come by and assist James for a couple of days after his surgery."

"Okay."

"She agreed, so that should really help us. The doctor said they wanted him to stay off his feet for a couple of days after the surgery. I thought it would be best to have a professional assist and check on him."

"She is the best." Sadie said with a proud smile.

"Yes she is, keep us all in your prayers, especially James."

"Of course Margaret. We have and will continue to pray for you and your family."

"Thanks."

"You are welcome." Kimberly and Sadie responded.

"Take care." Kimberly said with a wave.

Kimberly walked into her Sadie's house with her. She closed the door behind them.

"That's very sweet of you Kimmie."

"Thank you Granny. I hope he has a successful surgery and a speedy recovery. I only want the best for them.

"They have been through a lot but I believe God will see them through."

Kimberly nodded and smiled.

"Can I fix you something?"

"Yes Kimmie can you heat up my left over from last night? I am going to take a quick shower."

45

"Sure."

"Dee's probably gone but you can fix yourself and Damen a plate. There's more than enough food in there."

"Umm yummy! I will fix us some plates. Thanks."

"You're welcome, help yourself."

Sadie walked into the bathroom.

Kimberly walked into the kitchen, washed her hands and began to place the containers on the table. First she fixed Damen, Dee and her plate. Later she fixed Sadie's plate. She opted to save her plate for last, keeping it warm as she showered so that it was warm when she ready to eat.

Sadie walked out in her nightgown as Kimberly placed her plate on the table.

"I also prepared some tea."

"Awww thanks Sweetie."

"You're welcome." Kimberly smiled and gave Sadie a huge hug.

"Goodnight Granny I love you."

"I love you too. Drive safely Kimmie. Give me a call when you make it home."

"I will Granny."

Kimberly closed and locked the door before walking back to her car.

Once she arrived home, she immediately called her Grandmother to inform her that she'd safely made it home.

Chapter6

Joshua

Joshua packed the last of their things into the trunk of his truck. He looked on the porch at his two children. They were growing up fast. Josh gave a quick smile and beckoned for them. They ran down the stairs and he assisted them as they got into the truck.

Before driving off he looked at the home he and his wife had shared for almost ten years. Josh couldn't sell it. The house held too many sentimental and memorable memories. For now, Josh would rent it out as he and his children traveled to Chicago to be with his Mom and Dad. The doctor stated that they wanted to remove the tumors. They would test them to make sure they were not cancerous.

Josh recently lost his wife; he couldn't lose his father too. He didn't even want to fathom the idea. He shook his head and drove off. Once they arrived to Chicago, Josh parked the car. He looked at the back seat where his children slept. The brick bungalow looked smaller than he remembered. As a child the home always felt so big. Perhaps, it was because he was the only child. Josh had ample amount of space and attention. His mom was a stay home Mom, while his Dad worked two jobs. Nevertheless, he managed to make time for his son and wife.

Josh never had to look for role models, he had them at home. They both instilled religion and the importance of having a relationship with God. But Joshua now disregarded God and religion. His dad taught him to work hard, give his best, provide for and protect his family. His mother taught him patience, empathy, sacrifice and dedication. Josh loved his parents. He would do anything for them. He couldn't bear losing either one of them. Josh barely made it through Lisa's death. He took a deep breath. Josh looked up at the sky and thought. If only you were up there.

"Daddy, I gotta go pee-pee. Mia said in between yawns.

"Okay Sweetie." Josh got out of the truck and took Junior out of the car seat. Mia who was four, unsnapped her seat belt. Josh took Junior and Mia's hand. They walked up the stairs. Josh rang the doorbell.

"Who is it?" Josh heard his Mom ask.

"It's me and the kids Mom."

The door flung opened.

"Josh! Oh my goodness!" Margaret said with a huge smile, as she gave him a huge hug.

"Na Na!" Junior said.

Margaret looked down at Junior and Mia!

"Awww!" She picked up Junior and gave him a hug before putting him down. She bent down and looked at Mia who was looking at her. Margaret smiled and hugged her tightly.

"Granny's been missing her babies."

"We missed you to Granny." Mia replied.

They walked into the house.

"James!" Margaret called out.

Mia walked to the bathroom.

"James our babies are here."

"Say what honey?" James asked as he walked from the kitchen.

"Josh! James walked up to Josh and gave him a big hug. Josh and his father hugged for an extended amount of time. Margaret with eyes got wet as she fought off tears. *God please, don't let this be cancerous.* She thought to herself.

James looked at Junior.

"Boy you look just like your Dad at that age."

Junior smiled.

Margaret nodded her head. "I said that, the last time they were here. Remember at the Christmas dinner."

James smiled and nodded his head.

"It's great having you and the kids here. It means a lot to me son."

"We're glad to be here Dad."

Margaret smiled. "How was your drive here?"

"Not too bad. The drive from Minnesota to Chicago usually takes about 8 hours or so. I split the drive up. I didn't want the kids to get restless so half way here we stopped and slept at a hotel and ate breakfast before I finished driving the other half today. *The kids slept at the hotel.* Margaret thought.

"How did you sleep?" She asked.

"I slept alright Mom, but I'm sure I will sleep better tonight."Josh said with a smile.

"I hope so Hun."

Josh looked down at Mia who sat down next to him.

"You okay sweetie?"

"Um hmmm."

Junior was on the floor rolling his car that he carried with him everywhere.

"I am going to get dinner started. Would you like to help Mia?" Margaret asked.

"Can I help Granny daddy?"

"Sure sweetie, have fun."

Mia smiled and ran towards Margaret to the kitchen.

James looked at Josh.

"They're growing up so fast."

"Yes they are Dad, too fast. It's time to enroll Mia into preschool. Can you believe that?" Josh asked while shaking his head.

"Have you thought about a school?"

"I've narrowed it down to two schools, but I'm thinking about moving back to Chicago."

"That's great Josh! Wait . . . I hope this doesn't have anything to do with me."

"No dad, this is something I've been thinking about for some time now. Like you said, the kids are getting older. I want them around you and mom, I want to be around you too. I miss you guys."

"We miss you too Son."

"Josh honey!" Margaret called from the kitchen.

"Yes mom? Josh responded as he walked towards the kitchen.

"Honey, I thought I had enough eggs but I don't. Can you go to the store and grab me a dozen of eggs, milk and bread?"

"Sure mom."

'Go into my purse in the . . ."

"Mom don't worry, I got it."

"Thanks Honey."

"You're welcome mom. Bye sweetie. I'll be back." Josh said as he kissed Mia on the forehead.

"Bye daddy!"

"Don't worry your dad will look after Junior." Margaret said with a smile.

Josh went into the foyer and grabbed his jacket.

"Daddy where you goin?" Junior asked, running after Josh.

"I'm going to the store."

Junior pouted and looked up at Josh.

"I'll be back Junior."

"Yes Junior your dad will be back." James said as he picked Junior up and carried him to the living room.

Josh closed the door and walked to his truck.

Once at the store, he grabbed a loaf of bread before walking over to the eggs.

That can't be? Josh thought.

"Kim?"

Kim turned around.

"Josh?!" They hugged briefly.

He still looks the same, just a little more distinguished she thought.

"It's good to see you." Kim said with a smile.

Life's been good to her, Josh thought. *She's even more beautiful than before.*

"My mom told me you were a nurse, that's fitting." Josh said with a smile.

"How so?"

"You were always nurturing and caring."

"Why, thanks." Kimberly smiled.

"So how long are you in town?"

"Not sure. . . I'm contemplating moving back"

"Really?! Your parents would love that."

"I think I would too."

Silence. . .

"How are your children? You have two right?"

"Yeah, Mia, she's four and Junior he's two."

"Wow! I know they keep you busy."

"They do, but in a good way."

"I bet" Kimberly said with a smile.

"Kim it was nice seeing you. I gotta get back." Josh lowered his voice, "I don't want to be responsible for holding up dinner."

"Of course not" Kimberly responded.

Josh turned to leave.

"Kim?"

"Yes."

"Can I call you sometimes? I see you're engaged."

Kimberly looked a bit shocked.

Josh pointed to her ring. "It would be strictly platonic."

Kimberly looked down at her ring. She didn't want to cause friction between Damen and her. Yet, she couldn't stop thinking about all Josh had been through and as her granny stated, he could use extra support.

"Sure, why not." She responded.

Josh pulled out his cell phone and immediately called Kimberly's phone.

Her phone rang.

"It works." Josh said with a smile.

"That's correct; I will program your number now."

"Good. If you need me don't hesitate to call." Why did he just say that? He thought.

"Okay thanks." Kimberly said with a nod.

Josh did miss her but he was not looking for anything romantic. He'd broke her heart once, he didn't want to do it again. He would never fall in love with another woman again. Lisa held his heart and he never wanted to share it with another woman but his mom and daughter. They held his heart.

"Take care Josh, and if you need someone to talk to I'm here."

Josh smiled. "Bye Kim."

"Bye Josh." Kimberly walked away.

Josh finished getting the grocery and checked out. He loaded his grocery and hopped in his truck before heading to his parent's house. Once he arrived at the house, he thought, *two more days and we will know rather or not the tumors are cancerous.* He hoped the next few days hastily came and went.

Josh got out the truck, grabbed the bags and walked up stairs. The door quickly opened.

"Daddy!" Junior screamed as he hugged his dad's leg.

James reached for a bag.

"Don't worry Dad, we got it." He handed Junior a bag.

Junior smiled as they carried the bags into the kitchen.

"Thank you." Margaret said with a smile.

"No problem mom." Josh looked down at Mia who had a huge grin on her face.

"Mom how's your little helper?

"Mia looked up at Margaret intensely.

"She's fantastic!"

Mia laughed out loud.

"Granny can I help you tomorrow too?"

"Absolutely honey, you can help me every day that you're here."

Mia gave Margaret a hug.

Josh smiled as he unloaded the groceries.

"I got a few extra groceries as well."

"You didn't have to Josh."

"I know Mom, I wanted to. Guess who I bumped into while shopping?"

"Who?"

"Kim"

"Oh! Did she see you?"

"Yeah, we talked."

"This is the first time you've seen her in years right?"

"Yeah."

"She will be coming over to the house to help your Dad and I after his surgery."

"I didn't know that . . . she didn't mention that to me."

"She's going to come over once or twice a week for a month to assist.

"That should be helpful."

"Who is Kimberly?" Mia asked.

"A family friend" Margaret responded.

"She was one of your dad's best friends in high school."

"You had a girl best friend? Mia asked with a frown.

"Yeah, I did." Josh said as he nodded his head.

"I thought John was your best friend? Mia continued.

"He is. But as you get older sweetie your best friend will more than likely be a boy. Your mom was my best friend."

Mia looked a bit confused and smiled.

"Well, I'm going to let the two of you finish cooking."

"Okay Daddy."

Josh walked out and headed into the living room. His dad was sitting down reading. Junior immediately ran after Josh.

"That's your shadow." James stated. He had a mini-melt down when you left for the store. Your mom had to come and comfort him."

"Junior's very sensitive and emotional. He tends to be a little withdrawn."

"I see."

"He suffers from insomnia and still sleeps in the bed with me. I've tried to get him to sleep in his room but to no avail."

"Junior will grow out of it, he will have to, especially if you ever get married again."

"Not happening."

"Josh?!"

"Dad I believe you only have one true love in this life, everyone else is either a substitute or a settling, second best."

"Love can be complex but are you telling me that Lisa's the only woman you've been in love with?"

"You and mom met in college. You told me that you knew she was the one after your second date and look you've been married for forty-two years. When it's right, it's right. Don't look so sad dad, I had that with Lisa."

"Josh you're only twenty-eight years old and to hear you planning to spend the rest of your life alone, saddens me."

"Dad, I'm not alone. I got my kids, you and mom. That's enough for me."

"But your mom and I want be here forever and your kids will grow up and live their own lives."

"Dad you and Mom will be here a long time. My kids will visit me and I will visit them when I get lonely."

"So Lisa's your first and only true love?"

"Well she's not my first love that was Kim."

"Do you think Lisa would want you to stay a widow?"

"Dad you should not be thinking about me right now."

"You are always a priority. Do you remember what you told me when you and Kim were dating?"

"Ummm. . . I told you a lot of stuff."

"Yes you did. When the time is right I will remind you of what you said and why it was so profound."

Josh looked at his dad perplexed.

"You always were a critical thinker."

They both laughed. James looked at Josh.

"Son, I've been contemplating what they might tell me on Thursday but whatever they tell me I am leaving the situation in God's hand."

Chapter 7

Kimberly

Ring, Ring. Kimberly looked down at her phone. It read, "Josh."

"Hi Josh."

"Kim my dad has cancer."

"What?!" *Oh God no!* Kimberly thought.

"Wha . . . what did the doctor's say?" Kimberly continued.

"They said he has stage 2 cancer . . . I can't lose my dad Kim."

"You're not going to lose your dad. James is a fighter. He's going to beat this. . . Where are you?"

"I'm at the hospital. I'm on my way to your Grandmother's house to pick up my kids."

"I can drop you off."

"Thanks for the offer, I'll be okay."

"We could meet at Lexie's and grab a cup of coffee?" Kimberly frowned. She didn't drink coffee.

"Coffee? . . . No thanks. I really want to be alone right now. I need to get my head straight so that I can be there for my parents you know?"

"You are there for your parents. Sometimes your presence alone is enough."

"Kim. . ."

"I can ask my Granny to keep the kids a little longer, that way you can have some time alone to gather your thoughts."

"I'll be alright."

"Bye Josh. I'm going to call her now."

"Kim I'll call her, that way if she's not able to keep them longer I can go and get them."

"I will call you if she can't."

. . .

"Okay?"

"Yeah, call me if she can't."

"I will, I promise."

"Thanks"

"You are welcome."

Kimberly ended the call and immediately called her Granny.

"Hi Kim."

"Hello Granny. Josh just called me . ."

"Is everything okay?"

"James has cancer."

"Oh no!"

"Can you keep the kids a little longer? He needs time to process this."

"Absolutely! Oh my God I pray that God touches his body and strengthen their family.
Wow."

"Thanks Granny."

"You're welcome."

Kimberly hung up the phone. She got on her knees and began to pray. *God the
Almighty, I look to you, knowing that you are a healer and a strong tower. Your word
says, "Behold, I will bring it health and cure, and I will cure them and will reveal unto
them the abundance of peace and truth. You said that by your stripes we are healed.
Heal and touch James. Strengthen and comfort the entire Crawley family. In Jesus
name. Amen.*

Kimberly opened her eyes as Damen walked into the bedroom.

"Is everything okay?"

"I just found out that a family friend has cancer."

Damen looked at Kimberly with concern. "Sorry to hear that."

Kimberly got up.

"I know things have been a little strained against the two of us, especially with the whole

. . . you know . . . incident and this Toya and Dee thing hasn't made it any easier. But I

love you Kim. I'm here for you no matter what."

Kimberly nodded her head.

"Come here."

Kimberly walked towards Damen. He gave her a hug.

"Everything's going to be okay."

Kimberly laid on Damen and closed her eyes.

"Kim did you hear!" Dee walked into the bedroom. "Oh my bad, I should have knocked

but James has cancer."

Kimberly looked at Dee and said, "I know Josh told me."

"Josh?! OMG! I know he's a mess.

"He's trying to hold it together. But he's scared."

"Josh?" Damen asked.

"Yes his father has cancer." She could tell Damen wanted to say more but opted not.

"Have you talked to Margaret? Dee asked.

"No I haven't."

"That's messed up. James is a good man." Dee shook her head. "Wow. I'm gonna step

out for a while Kim. Keep me inform if you hear any new information."

"I will, be careful Dee."

"I will, later Kim."

"Later Dee, love you."

"Love you too Sis." Dee walked out of the bedroom.

Damen looked at Kim.

"I didn't know you kept in touch with Josh."

"We didn't. I ran into him two days ago at the market."

"And you gave him your number?"

"Yes, I wanted to be courteous. He is going through a lot, he lost his wife, his dad is ill . .
. "

"That's why I love you. You're so thoughtful and caring."

"You're not mad?"

"No. Should I be?"

"Of course not."

"Good because I don't do jealousy." Damen said with a smile.

"Yeah, you wouldn't wear jealousy well."

Damen laughed.

"Let's get outta here." Damen suggested.

"Where to?"

"My ranch."

"We can ride some horses, have a picnic and spend some much needed alone time."

"That sounds tempting, but I think it's better for me to stay in town for awhile."

"Are you sure?"

"I am . . . rain check?"

"I guess." Damen said with a smiled.

Chapter 8

Josh

Josh was distraught. He walked along the park trail just thinking. His dad was going to be okay. Right? Josh just felt so helpless, he wished there was something he could do. He looked down at his phone, it read, Mom"

"Hi Mom is everything okay?"

"Yes, I was checking on you."

"Mom I'm okay. How's Dad doing? "

"Your dad's doing well, a little too well."

"He's putting on face for us."

"I don't think so, he is really content. He is asking that God's will be done."

"Yeah, he's really putting a lot of emphasis on God."

"God is faithful."

"I hope he is more faithful to Dad than he was with Lisa."

"Josh God loves your dad and he loved Lisa."

" . . ."

"Josh?"

"I'm here mom."

"Josh . . . God is still God. It was very tragic the way you lost Lisa but God . . . "

"Mom the kids and I should be home in an hour or so. Should I bring something?" Josh asked, changing the subject.

"No love."

"If you need anything give me a call."

"I will love."

"Love you Mom."

"I love you too Josh."

Josh hung up the phone. He walked to his car and drove to Lexie's. Once in Lexie's he had a cup of coffee. Josh tried not to think about anything. He looked out the window and stared out for several minutes. After he finished his coffee, he felt somewhat better. Josh picked up his phone and called Sadie.

"Hey Josh."

"Hello Ms. Sadie. I am on my way to get the children now. I should be there in ten minutes."

"Okay Sweetie, I'll see you in a few minutes."

"Alright Ms. Sadie."

Once Josh arrived at Sadie's house he thanked her.

"Thanks Ms. Sadie."

"Don't mention it."

He came inside the house.

"Daddy!" Mia exclaimed as she hugged her dad.

"Where's Junior?"

"He's sleeping." Mia said with a smile.

Sadie went into the room and came out carrying a sleeping Junior.

Josh took him and extended money towards Sadie.

"Sadie pushed his hand and shook her head.

"I'm not taking that. I am here for you and your family. If I can be of any assistance, I'm just a call away, heck a few steps away. Your parents stay right across the street."

Josh cracked a smile.

"My family and I truly appreciate you."

"I know."

Josh kissed Sadie on the cheek, grabbed the children's bag before saying, "Good-bye."

Mia turned around, "Bye-bye."

"Bye sweetie."

Josh waved good-bye as he secured the children into their seats.

Once at his parents' house, he found them both sleeping. He gave his children their baths before tucking them into bed. He climbed into bed, hoping for some rest.

Chapter 9

Kimberly

Kimberly walked into her patient's room. She handed her a cup with her medicine and a fresh pitcher of ice water. The patient, Stephanie had a visitor, who was blatantly staring at Kimberly from the moment she walked into the room. Kimberly smiled and introduced herself.

"Hello, I'm Stephanie's nurse, Kimberly."

"Hello, I'm Stephanie's best friend."

"Nice to meet you."

The friend continued to stare at Kim.

Kimberly looked away from her and at Stephanie.

"Do you need anything Stephanie?"

"No thanks Kimberly, I'm fine."

"Kimberly closed the door and continued to do her rounds.

Once she was done, she headed back to the nurse's station where her coworkers, Sharon and Macy sat.

"Ladies I'm going to lunch."

"Okay Kim, tell that fine Damen I said hello." Macy said with a smile

Sharon shook her head. "Girl don't pay that Chile' no mind."

Kimberly smiled and waved her hand as she walked away.

****

Kimberly was surprised to see Josh in the cafeteria. She walked over,

"Do you mind if I join you?"

64

Kimberly asked as she sat down next to Josh.

"Suit yourself" Josh said with a slight smile. He looked as if he needed some rest.

"How are you?"

"I've been better." Josh raised his eyebrows and smiled. "But thanks for asking."

"Sure." Kimberly opened her Styrofoam container and picked up her fork.

"Daddy! Daddy! Grandma got me and Junior some ice cream."

"Nice!"

Kimberly looked up at the little girl who was staring at her.

She was beautiful.

"Hello."

"Who are you?" Mia asked

"I'm Kim, a friend of your dad."

"My dad has enough friends."

"Mia! That's not nice." Josh looked at Mia with a frown.

"Apologize to Kim."

"It' okay Josh."

"No, it's not okay for her to be rude. Mia?"

"I'm sorry." Mia said with a pout.

"I accept your apology Mia."

Margaret and Junior came to the table.

"Hi Kim! How are you?"

"I'm good Mrs. Margaret. How are you?

"I'm doing okay."

Kimberly looked at the little boy with his head down and her heart just melted. He was standing next to Margaret. Junior had to be Josh's clone.

"Hello." Kimberly started, "You must be Junior?"

Junior looked up at her and nodded his head.

"You like icey cream?" Junior asked.

"I love ice cream. What's your favorite kind of ice cream?"

"Chocolate."

"Yum, great choice." Kimberly said with a smile.

Josh smiled.

Mia took Junior's hand and walked him away from Kimberly and towards Margaret.

She really doesn't like me Kimberly thought.

"Why don't we go check on Grandpa?" Margaret said.

"Can I stay with Daddy?" Mia asked.

"Your dad will join us a little later Mia." Margaret smiled at Josh and Kimberly as she took the kids.

"You have beautiful kids." Kimberly said with a smile.

"Thanks."

Kimberly ate some of her lunch.

"So . . . do you still dream of flipping properties?"

"Honestly, I haven't really given it much thought."

"You've been through a lot, its understanding."

Josh looked at her. "Do you still want four children?"

"What?!" You still remember that?"

Josh nodded his head. "Yes I do."

Kimberly smiled. "Well, I'm not a spring chicken anymore so . . . No!"

"You're only twenty-seven."

"Yeah, but, back then I was young and loved the idea of having a big family."

"Aside from Lisa, Mia and Junior are the best things that's happened to me." "Children are a blessing."

"Yeah, if you believe in blessings, miracles, God and all the religious terminology used for time and chance."

Kimberly was taken aback. She and Josh prayed often, while dating. They even talked about the importance of keeping God first. They even promised to keep God first in their marriage.

". . . I didn't know you felt that way." Kimberly was disappointed.

"I've changed, I'm not the Josh you knew in high school."

"We've grown. I'm not the same as high school either but I remember you having strong faith. I always admired that in you."

Josh smiled. "You were always the glass half full type of girl. Something tells me that hasn't changed. "

"Perhaps." Kimberly winked.

"And something tells me that everything is going to work out for you and your family."

"I hope so."

Josh looked at his watch.

"I better get going."

"Take care of yourself Josh."

Josh lifted his hand and waved good-bye."

Kimberly finished her lunch and headed back to work.

Chapter 10

Josh

Josh walked into his father's room. His mom and children were looking at the television. His dad was asleep. Junior immediately gave him a hugged. Mia looked at him.

"We're watching Doc McStuffins, wanna watch it too daddy?"

"Sure princess." Josh said with a smile. Margaret looked at Josh. "How's Kimberly? Did you two catch up a bit?"

"She's doing well and we did catch up a bit but don't go getting any ideas."

"What?!"

"I know you mom."

"Daddy you're not watching." Mia complained.

"Sorry princess." Josh smiled as he looked at his mom.

Margaret smiled and whispered, "Possessive."

They watched two episodes of Doc McStuffins. James opened his eyes.

"Well hello, nobody told me there was going to be a party in my room. I would have stayed awake."

Mia gave him a hug.

"Do you need anything Dad?"

"No son I'm good."

Margaret fluffed his pillows a bit before sitting back down.

"They should be serving you dinner soon it's almost five."

James nodded, "I am getting a bit hungry. I slept for awhile."

"You needed that rest dad."

"I guess I did."James gave a quick laugh. "How's my grandbabies doing?"

"We're fine, Papa." Mia said with a smile.

Josh and his children stayed at the hospital until visiting hours were over. Josh walked over to his dad and kissed his forehead.

"I love you dad, I'll see you in the morning."

James looked at Josh and nodded his head.

"Okay Son, see you tomorrow."

"Bye Papa! Mia said.

"Bye Mia and Junior."

Junior waved good bye. "Bye Papa."

Josh hugged his mom and gave her a kiss on the cheek.

"Bye Mom. I'll see you in the morning."

"Bye honey."

"I'll call you and check on the two of you tonight, once I've gotten the children settled."

"Okay honey, I'll talk to you tonight."

"Love you."

"Love you too Josh."

****

Josh rolled over after hearing the alarm go off. He got up and checked on the kids, they were sleeping. Josh hopped in the shower before starting breakfast. His dad was having surgery today in hopes of removing all of the cancerous tumors. Josh was a nervous wreck. He just hoped it didn't show around his mom and dad. He walked over and sat the eggs, pancakes and sausages on the table.

"Daddy."

Josh looked down at his son who was staring up at him with bags underneath his eyes. Junior suffered from insomnia. He had talked to his pediatrician; her solution was light medication, relaxation techniques and observations. Josh didn't like the idea of giving him medication so he opted for the relaxation techniques; they assisted some but not always. Last night Junior got about four hours of sleep. Josh bent down.

"How are you feeling kiddo?"

"Okay." Junior said while standing on his tip toes looking at the table. Josh picked him up; allowing him to view what was on the table. Junior smiled.

"Pancakes!"

Pancakes were Junior's favorite. Junior smiled and hugged his dad's neck. Josh put him down.

"Come on let's wake Mia so we can eat breakfast." Junior grinned and nodded his head.

 They walked into Mia's room.

Junior immediately ran over to her.

"Mia! Mia!"

Mia rolled over and opened her eyes.

"Pancakes, pancakes Mia!" Junior exclaimed.

Mia climbed out of bed.

"Okay, okay Junior." Mia responded.

"Come on let's wash your hands for breakfast."

Josh encouraged as they immediately followed behind him to wash their hands.

They sat at the table.

"Daddy can we say grace?" Mia asked.

Josh looked bewildered.

"We say grace with Granny and Ms. Sadie."

"Princess . . ." Josh started. ". . . Sure."

Mia grinned and held her head down.

Josh hoped she wasn't waiting on him. Mia looked up at Josh.

"Daddy are you ready?"

"I am Princess. Why don't you show me how you say grace?"

"Me?!" Mia asked astonishingly.

"Yes."

"Umm . . . Okay . . . God thank you for this breakfast. Thank you Daddy for making it, especially the pancakes! Please make it healthy for our bodies and touch PaPa. Amen."

"A man." Junior replied

Josh was amazed at how much she learn about grace and prayers in such a short period of time.

"Princess you did a great job on saying grace."

"Thank you Daddy." Mia said with a huge grin on her face.

"Pancakes!" Junior said with a huge smile.

"Okay, here comes the pancakes."

* * * *

Josh scurried from the parking lot to the hospital's main entrance. He looked at his watch; he had about fifteen minutes before they began the surgery prep for his dad. Once he made it in the room he saw his mom, his dad and Kim all in a circle praying. *I'll wait until this is over, but, if You are up there, have mercy on my dad."* Once they finished prayer, Josh greeted everyone.

"Good afternoon."

"Hi Baby." Margaret greeted as she kissed him on the cheek.

"Hi son!" James said with a smile.

"Today's the big day." James continued.

"How are you feeling?" Josh asked.

"Very optimistic about it." James said with a smile.

"I've better get going." Kimberly said with a smile. "It's nice seeing you Josh."

"Same here Kim."

Kimberly gave Margaret a hugged before grabbing James hands.

"Don't you worry, everything is going to be alright.

"I know Kimmie, I know."

Kimberly gave a slight smile as she walked towards the door.

"Kim!" Josh called. "Can I talk to you for a minute?"

"Sure."

Josh walked outside.

"In your honest opinion is Dr. Walker the best doctor for this procedure? I've read the success rate and reviews from patients and Dr. Haymore has better reviews. You work here so your perspective's more insightful. I know ..."

"Josh . . ."

"Hear me out, I know it's a little late, but I want my dad in the best hands. I value your opinion."

"Josh, in my honest opinion, Dr. Walker is the best for this procedure. Not only is he a great surgeon, his faith in God is tremendous. If my life was on the line, I would want him holding the scalpel."

Josh sighed. "Then Dr.Walker it is."

Kimberly smiled and hugged Josh. He held her for a few seconds and whispered,

"Thanks Kim."

Kimberly looked up at him.

"You're welcome." *God's working this out.* Kimberly thought. "Let me know when he's out of surgery."

Josh nodded "I will."

Kimberly waved, "See you later."

"Later." Josh gave a slight grin.

Chapter 11

Damen

Damen was anxious. He had shared the news with his mom, now he needed to tell Kimberly. He had no doubt, she would be happy for him but would she'd agree? Damen knew Kim would do just about anything for him, but this was different.

Damen walked into their condo where he saw Dee sitting on the sofa watching TV.

"Hello." Damen greeted as he closed the door.

"Hi Damen?! You're home early. What's up?"

"Prospective promotion."

"Shouldn't that require more hours?"

"It does, just like job hunting requires hunting for a job." Dee rolled her eyes and shook her head as Damen walked into the kitchen. *Perhaps it was time for Kim and him to set a wedding date.* He thought as he drank some water.

Several minutes later Kimberly walked in.

"Hi Dee; is Damen here?"

"Hey Sis, yeah he got here like ten minutes ago. He's on the phone in the bedroom and before you worry yourself crazy, he is fine."

"Thanks Dee."

"Don't look so worried."

Kim walked into the bedroom. Damen was on the phone looking out the window. He turned around when he heard the door open. Damen smiled and lifted his head to greet Kimberly.

"Let me call you back." He ended the call.

"Are you okay Babe?" Kimberly asked.

"It depends on your response."

"What are you talking about? Kimberly asked with a smile.

"I've been offered partnership . . ."

"What?! That's great!" Kimberly hugged Damen.

"Here's the thing, it's in New York. Our firm's extending to New York."

"New York?" Kimberly asked.

"Yes, I want you to come to New York with me?"

"Uhh . . ."

"Hear me out, I know it's a lot to ask of you, being how close you are to your Grandma and Dee but we could get a house with enough room for them. I don't want to go without you."

". . ."

Damen stared at Kimberly in anticipation.

"Yes Damen, I will move to New York with you."

"What?! Sweet!" Damen said with a smile as he hugged her.

"That's awesome! Let me call Dave and let him know my answer is yes."

"You were going to turn down making partner for me?

"Absolutely!"

"Awww! I love you."

"I love you too."

"When are we moving?"

"In about a month and five days."

"Okay." Kimberly nodded her head. Damen could tell she was trying to take it all in.

"You're going to love it, I'll see to it."

Kimberly smiled.

Damen looked down at his phone, "This is Dave." Kimberly nodded. "I am going to share the news with Dee.

"Okay Doll." Damen answered the phone. "Hi Dave, I accept. I am going to go for it."

Chapter 12

Kimberly

Kimberly walked out of the bedroom into the living room where Dee was watching tv.

Dee looked up at Kimberly. "Kim is everything okay?"

Kimberly nodded. "Damen got a job promotion and it's in New York."

"New York?!"

"Yes."

"You're not planning on going with him are you?"

"I am."

"Wow . . . what am I going to do without my big sister?"

"I am still going to be here for you no matter what. That's what family's for."

"When are you moving?"

"Damen said in about a month."

"How are you feeling about the move? I know how much you love your job."

"I am going to miss my coworkers and patients but I'm going to apply for a nursing job in New York. . . I will come back and visit them but it's going to be hard. I'm going to miss you and Granny the most, I know we'll visit each other but I am going to miss our face to face conversations."

"Have you told Grandma yet?"

"I haven't, Damen just told me. I am going to stop by her house and tell her."

"Good luck with that!"

Kimberly smiled.

"I am going over to Granny's house to talk to her." Kimberly said with a smile.

Dee smiled.

"Dee even though we are moving, you can come stay with us if you like."

"No thanks! I hope to have found a job and a place by then."

"I'm sure you will. I just wanted you to know that."

Damen walked out of the bedroom.

"We are all set; they're offering $45,000 for a down payment on a house."

"Wow! That's great babe!"

"It is."

"I am going to Granny's and tell her the news."

"Okay, but no reneging."

Kimberly smiled. "I won't."

"Tell me Doll, do you want a big wedding or small one?"

Kimberly looked a bit bewildered.

"Small."

"Let Ms. Sadie know that we'll be Mr. & Mrs. Moore before we move."

"Really? I'm not telling her that until we have a date set."

"How about the third Saturday of this month."

"Let's do it!"

"Kim!"Dee interjected

"That's not enough time!"

"Not enough time for the two of us but we got you and you are awesome with details . .
."

"And spreading news." Damen added.

Dee rolled her eyes.

"Whatever Damen, we all know you're only setting the date to secure Kimberly moving

to New York with you."

"What would I do without you two?" Kimberly shook her head as she kissed Dee on the forehead.

"Bye Babe." Kimberly kissed Damen and waved goodbye.

****

"Hi Granny, how are you?"

"I'm good sweetie."

"Daddy!" Junior exclaimed as he ran into the living room."

"No sweetie, this is my baby."

"No, no." Junior said with a slight smile.

"Hi Junior."

Junior looked up at Kimberly, "Hello." He said softly before holding his head down as he walked back towards the kitchen behind Sadie. Mia was at the kitchen table drawing.

"Hi Mia."

Mia looked at Kim.

"I remember you, you were talking to my dad."

"I was, it's nice seeing you again."

"Were you with my Dad?"

"No, I just left my house. Your Dad's at . . .

"The hospital, I know."

Sadie glanced over at them briefly.

"I'm going to sit him on the potty. I will be back.

"Okay Granny."

"You know Ms. Sadie too?"

"She's my Grandma. I know your Grandma and Grandpa too."

Mia looked away. "You're following me."

"I wasn't trying to follow you but I'm happy to see you again."

"Why?"

"Because you are beautiful and sweet."

"How do you know I'm sweet?"

"Because you look after your Dad."

Kim could tell she wanted to smile but didn't want her to see her.

Sadie and Junior walked back into the kitchen.

"Did he pee?!" Mia asked.

"No, he didn't want to sit on toilet." Sadie responded.

"Yeap that's what he does to my Daddy." Mia nodded. "My Daddy took him to the potty

and told him he could stand up." Mia shook her head.

"He'll learn soon." Sadie said with a smile.

Sadie began to prepare their snacks.

"I can help." Kimberly stated.

Sure can you make sure Junior washes his hands with soap?

Kimberly walked over towards Junior.

"Can I help you wash your hands?"

Junior nodded.

Once Kimberly finished assisting Junior with his hand washing, she washed her hands

and they walked to the kitchen.

Sadie then placed their plates in front of them.

"Thank you." Junior said as he quickly grabbed his sandwich and took a bite.

"Thank you Ms. Sadie." Mia said with a smile.

"You're welcome."

Kimberly joined them for snacks. She observed Mia's confidence as she talked to Ms. Sadie. Mia only said a few words to Kimberly when she asked her questions. Junior on the other hand, was very quiet and observant. He smiled at Kimberly several times as he ate his snack.

"You like turtles?" Junior asked.

"Ninja turtles?" Kimberly asked curiously.

"Umm hmm and crawling turtles!" He said with his eyes dilated and a huge grin.

Kimberly laughed.

"He loves turtles." Mia stated.

"How about you Mia. What do you like?"

"Doggies, I love doggies."

"Nice. Big dogs or small ones?"

"Small ones for your purse."

Kimberly laughed.

Just then the doorbell rang.

"Granny I'll get the door."

"Okay, thanks sweetie."

Kimberly walked to the door.

"Who is it?" Kimberly asked.

"Josh."

Kimberly opened the door.

"Hi Josh."

"Kim?"

"How did everything go?"

"The surgery went well." Josh said with a smile. "Now we just have to wait. Hopefully, no more tumors."

"There will be no more tumors."

"We hope not."

"No more tumors." Kimberly shook her head.

Josh smiled. "No more tumors."

"Now you're talking."

"Daddy!" Junior exclaimed as he ran toward his dad.

"Hey son!" Josh said as he scooted down and hugged his son.

Ms. Sadie and Mia followed after Junior from the kitchen.

"Hey Daddy!" Mia said.

"Hey Princess."

"Hello Miss. Sadie."

"Hi Josh how are you?"

"I'm actually good."

"Oh that's great! I love to hear that. So James is doing well?"

"Yes he is, the surgery went well."

"Thank God!" Ms. Sadie gleam.

Josh smiled. "Thank you Ms. Sadie for taking care of the kids. You are very supportive and my family and I appreciate you."

"Josh you are welcome. I told you if your family needed anything I would help."

"Can I offer you a monetary thanks?"

"Nope!"

"She's not going to take it Josh."

Josh smiled. "Kim thanks for your support as well. Can I treat you to a cup of hot chocolate or coffee? "

"You don't owe me anything Josh."

"Well I want to."

Sadie quickly interrupted. "Kim it's just a cup of hot chocolate to say thanks. It would be nice."

"Do you drink coffee now? I was surprised when you invited me for coffee a few weeks ago."

"No." Kimberly laughed. "Coffee was the first thing that came out. I wanted to cheer you up and I remembered how much loved coffee. It just came out."

"I see."

"I can even keep the kids." Sadie quickly suggested.

Josh smiled. "Thank you Ms. Sadie."

"No problem. She'll go with you. Right Kimmie? "

Kimberly looked at Sadie and shook her head. "Sure, I'll go. How does Thursday at noon sound?"

"That works for me, see you then."

"See you Thursday."

Josh looked at his children.

"Alright kids let's go."

"Bye Ms. Sadie, bye Kim." Mia said with a wave.

"Bye." Kimberly and Ms. Sadie said in unison.

Junior waved at Sadie and gave Kimberly a hug.

"Bye-bye." He said with a smile.

Josh looked astonished as he smiled at his son and Kimberly.

"Bye sweetheart."

****

Today was Thursday and Kimberly's off day. She slept later today. Damen told her not to bother with making him breakfast. He said he would grab something on the way so that she could stay in bed a little longer. Kimberly appreciated that. She hopped in the shower before stepping out the bedroom. The door immediately opened.

"What are you wearing?" Dee asked without knocking.

Kimberly shook her head.

"Have you ever heard of knocking?"

"Nope, not when it's my sister's room."

"Well, I'm going to wear this long, blue and white maxi dress. Why?"

"Emmm . . . I don't know about that one. . . I was thinking about that little black dress, you wore when you were trying to impress Damen."

"What?! No."

"This is your ex, if you don't want him anymore at least make him hate that he let you go."

"Nope, not interested in doing that"

"You know you want to, Miss. Goodie too shoes."

"Stop it Dee! You know that's not true."

"Whatever. Hey! You never told me what Granny said about you moving to New York with Damen."

"Actually, Granny took it well. I started the conversation with Granny, Damen and I have set our wedding date for June 20th, and after we get married he and I are moving to New York because he has job promotion in New York. I love you and I hope you can accept my decision."

"What?! And what did Granny say?"

"She said, Kimmie you know I love you and I wish nothing but the best for you and Damen."

"What?! Am I the team Josh alone?"

"What are you talking about? Damen and I are getting married? There's no team Josh."

"Getting married, not married but can you at least wear the hot pink one?"

"No." Kimberly threw and hit her with a pillow. "I am wearing this one."

"Boring!"

Kimberly put the dress on, ignoring Dee. She pulled the dress down.

"Oh wow, it looks better on you. However, you still should have worn the black or hot pink dress for this occasion."

Kimberly pulled her hair up in a high bun, applied light make up and placed some medium hoop earrings in her ears.

"You look great Sis." Dee said with a smile.

"Thanks Sis."

"You're welcome. Have fun."

****

Kimberly walked into Lexie's. Josh was already sitting down. Kimberly waved as she walked over towards him.

"Hi Josh! How are you?"

"I'm good. How are you?"

"I'm great."

Josh stood up and pushed in Kimberly's chair. Josh looked nice. He didn't have the heavy bags under his eyes that he recently wore whenever Kimberly saw him. He had on a pair of jeans and a blue Polo shirt. Kimberly smiled as she sat down.

"I've missed you Kim." Josh said seriously.

Oh no he didn't! Kimberly thought. *Where did that come from?*

"That was random."

"I know, but I've always been transparent with you."

"Except for when you ended things with me. I didn't see that coming."

"I know and I apologize for that. You were always honest and supportive. I should have not ended things that way."

"That was the past I hold no ill feelings towards you."

Josh stared at her.

The waitress came over and asked them what they'd like to drink before she quickly came back with their drinks.

"So tell me, what's your fiancé like?"

"Pardon?" Kimberly asked.

"Your fiancé, what's he like?"

"He's smart, spontaneous, confident and kind."

"Does he make you happy?"

"Absolutely! . . . I'm sorry this is a little awkward."

"Why?"

"Hmmmm, let me see, you don't talk about your fiancée to your ex. It's just weird."

"How about trying to see me as your friend? I don't want to be your ex, I want to be a friend."

"Fair enough."

"How did you know he was the one?"

"There's a feeling that I get whenever he's around. I can't wait to get home and share my days and evenings with him, talking, going out or just cuddling.

Just little things like that. How did you know Lisa, that was her name right?"

Josh nodded his head.

"How did you know Lisa was the one?"

"I fell in love with her free spirit and caring ways. You know I'm serious; she made me laugh and loosen up, like you. She kinda reminded me of you."

Kimberly was speechless. She didn't know how to respond.

"The chicken fettuccine alfredo is delicious!"

Josh gave a slight laugh. "Anything else you recommend?"

"What are you in the mood for? Pasta, sandwich, salad, oh! I forgot."

"Salad's rabbit food." They said in unison as they laughed out loud.

"Just a good sandwich." Josh answered.

"Oh then, the BBQ double bacon burger."

"Now that sounds enticing." Josh said with a smile.

The waitress came over and took their orders.

Chapter 13

Joshua

Joshua stared at Kimberly. She was even more beautiful now than in high school. When she walked into Lexie's, it was reminiscent of the very first time he saw her. She walked with confidence yet there was a bit of uncertainty in her eyes. When he first met Kimberly it was at lunch. She walked over to their table at lunch and said, "Hello do you all mind if I sit with you?" Kimberly had several classes with Josh's friend, Karen. Karen immediately responded, "Sure you can join us."

He and Kimberly hit it off quickly with their love for God, family and music. Kimberly pointed out that they had attended the same church for years. She had remembered him, but he had not noticed her, probably because he was infatuated with Tameka Kilson. When he ended things with Tameka, Kimberly reassured him that he'd done the right thing. She was always there for him rather he won a game or lost a game. And he definitely wasn't the easiest person to get along with, after he lost a game. Kimberly respected him and was not trying to be his friend because of the perks like Tameka and a few others from their school. He liked that about her. They started dating. As they got more serious, Josh wanted to take things further by becoming intimate but Kimberly reminded him of their very first conversation when they started dating. She was saving herself for marriage. Though difficult he respected that. Even when Kimberly came to him after rumors around school suggested that he and Tameka had messed around after the football celebration that Kimberly could not attend. She asked him if it was true. Josh admitted that she flirted with him at the party. He informed her that Tameka left the party after him and asked him for a ride, of which he agreed. Tameka continued to flirt with him during the car ride. Although, tempted, he dropped her off at her house and left.

Josh told Kimberly he left because he loved and respected her to much to betray her like that. Kimberly walked up to him and said, "I love you too." Kimberly kissed Josh and said, "I know I told you we'd wait . . . but . . ."
Josh remembered looking Kimberly in her eyes and saying, "I've waited for you three years, I can wait until we're married."
Kimberly looked relieved and happy as she hugged him and said, "I know you are the one God made for me."

"Josh?!" Kimberly was waving her hand in front of Josh. "Where did you just go? I called you several times."
"I'm sorry."
Kimberly smiled and shook her head.
Just then the waitress came to the table with their meals.
"Thank you." Kimberly said to the waitress with a smile.
Kimberly closed her eyes and bowed her head. Josh remembered how they would hold hands and pray over their food whenever they ate. Josh began to eat. Kimberly opened her eyes.
"You were right about BBQ burger it's delicious!"
Kimberly nodded. "I always order that one, when I want a burger."
"I can see why." Josh said nodding his head. "Would you like a piece?"
"It's tempting but I'm gonna work on this." Kimberly said as she pointed to her large chicken salad.
"More for me."Josh said with a wink. Kimberly laughed as she ate her salad.

"So, are you still an avid sox fan?"

"Absolutely! I'm going to miss the home games when we move."

"You're moving?"

"Yes, Damen and I are moving to New York, next month."

"New York? Interesting how did Ms. Sadie take it?"

"She took it well. Why?"

"Because you were always her baby."

"What! No."

"Yeah, whatever she asked of you, you did it and she loved you for it."

"I don't think so but I was quite surprised she took it so well. I had already prepared my rebuttal but she took it well. That was comforting I wouldn't want to leave if she had a hard time with it."

"You would not move if she'd openly disagreed with your decision to move."

"You're right."

"You've always been Grandma's baby."

Kimberly shook her head "I do love and respect her opinion dearly. She took care of Dee and I when we were one and two years old, after our parents died in the car crash. I wish I could take them both with me to New York. Selfish right?"

"Not selfish. You're being inclusive. However, it's important to keep in mind that they have their lives, jobs and homes here, in Chicago."

"I know."

"I'm going to miss you."

"No you're not!" Kimberly playfully hit his arm.

"Why do you think I'm lying?"

Just then a lady walked over to the table.

"Hi, you may not remember me but . . ."

"I remember you. We met at the hospital . . . you're Stephanie's friend right?"

"Yes. Is this your fiancé? "

"No, this is my friend Josh."

"Hi, nice to meet you." Josh said with a smile.

"I'm great! It's a pleasure meeting you."

She said with a smile. Well I've better get going. Nice seeing you again Kim . . . right?"

"Yes. How's Stephanie? "

"She's good."

"That's good, tell her I said hello."

"I will. You two take care. Nice meeting you Josh."

"Same here."

Kimberly lifted her eyebrows. "Somebody's got their eyes on you."

"What?! No, I doubt it."

"Look I'm a woman and I know when a woman's attracted to a man."

"Well I'm a man and I didn't see that."

"You guys rarely do."

"Are you talking from experience?"

"Maybe, maybe not."

"Tell me more."

"I'm no expert, but she definitely had her eyes on you." Kimberly said with a laugh.

"Actually, she stared more at you than me."

They both laughed.

"Stop it! Kimberly stated.

"It still doesn't change the fact that she finds you attractive."

Josh shook his head.

"So have you dated anyone since Lisa's . . ."

"You can say it."

"Since Lisa's death."

"No I haven't. I'm not interested in dating. I got my kids and parents."

Kimberly nodded her head.

Why did she look shock? Josh thought.

"I see." Kimberly said.

"I've been in love twice. I'm satisfied with that."

Kimberly smiled. "I better get going Josh it's getting late."

Kimberly looked at her watch and signaled for the waitress.

"This was nice." She said with a smile.

"It was, we have to do this again before you move."

"Absolutely!"

"How about a sox game?"

"I'd love it! We could invite a few people. Damen loves sports."

"Yeah." Josh felt a hint of Jealousy.

"Ring! Ring!" Josh looked down at his phone. It was his Mom.

"Give me one minute let me answer this."

"Sure." Kimberly said with a nod.

"Hello?"

"Hi Daddy!"

"Hi Princess!"

"Where are you?"

"I'm having lunch with a friend."

"Is it Kimberly?"

"Yes, but we are almost done."

"Good, cause we don't want to lose you."

The waitress placed the bill on the table. Josh took it.

"Lose me?! Princess I'm not going anywhere. Where did you get that idea?"

"If you keep going out with Kimberly, you won't be with me and Junior."

"Princess, no one will keep me from spending time with you and Junior."

"I have to go, Nana's coming."

"Nana doesn't mind if you talk to me."

"Yeah, yeah, she told me not to call you. Gotta go,love you!"

"Click."

Josh shook his head.

"Is everything okay?"

"Yeah, it was my daughter."

The waitress came over to the table. Josh handed her the bill.

"I think that's nice how Mia looks after you.

Josh smiled. "She something else."

He walked Kimberly to her car before going to his car.

****

Josh walked into his parents' house humming.

It was surprisingly quiet. The house was rarely silent with Mia and his mom.

"Hi Baby. I haven't seen you like this in awhile. I take it that you had a good time?"

"Mom I had a great time. She's so easy to talk to. Being with Kim is easy. I missed that."

93

Margaret smiled. "She's a sweet, genuine girl."

"She is. She's moving to New York."

"What?! When?"

"Next month."

"Sadie didn't even tell me!"

"I think this decision was recently made."

"Perhaps so, I'm going to miss her."

"I know, I'm going to miss her as well."

Chapter 14

Kimberly

Kimberly opened the front door. Dee immediately turned from the TV and greeted her.

"Hi Kim! So how did everything go?"

"It was nice."

"Nice, come on girl, you've got to give me more details than that."

"Josh was more at ease today, less stressed. It was nice to see him that way."

"So what was he wearing? Was there any flirting going on?"

"Actually there was."

"Ha! I knew it!"

"How did it start?"

"It wasn't between Josh and I. One of my patient's friend had her eyes on Josh. He didn't see it and made a joke of it."

"Probably because he only has his eyes for you."

"No, Josh isn't looking to date anyone. He told me this."

"That's what his mouth says but his actions are singing another tune."

"What was he wearing?"

"A pair of blue jeans and a blue polo shirt."

"You checked him out I see."

What?!"

"Yeah, that's what I said. What was the girl wearing that you said was flirting with him?"

"I don't remember."

"Exactly!"

"Dee!" Kimberly said shaking her head.

"I'm going to get dinner started."

"You are a good one. You cook for Damen 4x's a week and you're not even his wife.

Girl you are whipped! "

"Not whipped, just in love. I like cooking."

"I don't buy that. What woman likes slaving over a hot stove? Not me that's for sure.

Does he even say thank you?"

"Yes, all of the time."

Dee shook her head. "So what's on the menu tonight?"

"Steak, homemade mashed potatoes, asparagus and banana pudding for dessert."

"Girl, I'm starving just hearing the menu."

Kimberly laughed. "On my days off from work, I like to treat him to a nice meal."

"Yeah, I'll help you peel the potatoes."

"Awww ... thanks Dee."

"You're welcome; we can talk more about your lunch date with Josh."

"No date, just lunch."

"Okay, your lunch outing with Josh."

Kimberly shook her head."There's no winning with you, is it?"

"Nope."

Kimberly continued to cook and Dee assisted.

Once everything was done, Kimberly looked at Dee.

"Well, I'm gonna take a quick shower. Damen should be here in ten minutes."

"Okay wifey."

Kimberly smiled. Dee always teased her and called her wifey when she did as Dee put

it, "wifey duties," such as cooking, cleaning, doing his laundry and packing his lunch.

Once out of the shower, Kimberly placed on a long orange dress with spaghetti stripes and placed her hair up, leaving two pieces of hair down on each side of her face. She heard the door opened and smiled. Kimberly walked out of the master bedroom into the living room, where she saw Damen.

"Hey doll." Damen said as he placed his brief case down and loosened his tie. "It smells delicious in here." Kimberly walked up to him and gave him a kiss.

"How was your day Babe?"

"Good, my closing remarks definitely swayed the jury if the evidence didn't. Sometimes, I impress myself with just how good I am."

"Don't get too cocky." Kimberly said with a smile. "But you are awesome babe."

"So are you." Damen pulled her close."Are we alone?"

"No Dee's in her room. Aren't you hungry?"

Damen kissed Kimberly. "Not that hungry." He said with a smile. His phone started vibrating. He looked down at it with a frown.

"Is everything okay?"

"Umm hmm." Damen said as he continued looking at his phone.

Kimberly walked to the kitchen and began to set the table. Dee came out of her bedroom. "So are we ready to eat?" Dee asked as she looked at Damen, who was still with his phone. Dee looked at Kimberly. "Did he see this meal?"

"He did, he's finishing up."

Just then Damen walked over to the table. "Okay, I'm done." They held hands while saying grace before passing the food.

"So what did you do today?"

"I went to lunch with Josh, did some grocery shopping, came home and prepared dinner. "

Dee looked at Damen with a smirk, when Kimberly told him about her lunch date with Josh, only to see him looking down at his phone. "That's nice." He said still looking down at his phone. Kimberly could tell he was preoccupied with his phone because normally he would have caught that.

"How was lunch? Did you two go to Lexie's?"

"Yeah, we did. How did you know?"

"You said that was you and Josh's favorite place to go when you dated, so I figured there."

"He listens." Dee said with a nod.

"He's a great listener, even when I think he's not paying attention, like now. . . Babe!

"I'm putting it away." Damen placed his phone in his pocket. "Dee what did you do today?"

"I filled out job applications, watched some TV, and assisted Kim with dinner. I did fill out job applications; I know that's what you're trying to figure out."

"Actually, I was starting a conversation. My sister, Cam, got an opening at her job. I told her about you. She's the owner of Petkare. It's a doggy day care."

"Oh heck no! I hate dogs!"

"Dee you will have no contact with the animals. You will be a receptionist. There's a huge desk where the receptionist sits, the dogs would have to jump to reach the top; you're safe. The pay is $12 an hour. It's yours if you want it."

"Really?! Oh wow. Yeah, I want it. When can I start? "

"I'll have to check with Cam but I think next week."

"Thanks Damen."

"You're welcome."

Kimberly smiled.

This is delicious; I think you're getting better at this." Damen said playfully.

"Thank you; I've had the perfect guinea pig." Kimberly smiled.

Damen's phone vibrated again and he turned his phone off.

"What's going on with you and that phone?!" Kim asked a bit agitated.

"I'm sorry Doll; the office won't let me be. There's this new case, they want me to take

on, it's a high profile case but it would require me out of state for a month or so. I told

them I would pass. During that time I'd be a newlywed, enjoying my honeymoon. I

guess I have to say it more firmly."

Dee lifted her eyebrow and continued eating.

"Do you want to take on this case?" Kimberly asked.

"No there'll be others."

"I asked because we could push the wedding back, that way it . . ."

"Absolutely not! No." Damen shook his head. "There will be other opportunities.

 Nothing comes before us Doll "

Kimberly smiled and nodded her head.

They finished dinner and Kimberly brought out the dessert. They continued laughing

and talking. Kimberly started collecting their plates. "I'll start cleaning this up."

Damen turned his phone back on.

"I think they got the message now. I'm going to take a shower and Doll, dinner was

delicious.

"Thanks Damen."

"You're welcome."

"And thanks for looking out for Dee with the job. I am the luckiest girl in the world!"

Kimberly said with a smile.

"I am pretty awesome but you're not too bad yourself."

Kimberly pushed her hair up and playfully cleared her throat, "Why thank you"

Damen smiled and walked into the bedroom.

Chapter 15

Damen

Damen could not believe Toya! Why was she constantly calling his phone like that? If he wasn't a good liar, she could have caused problems for him and Kim. He looked down at the last text message that stated, *Damen you can't keep ignoring me. I am on my way to your house; let's see how your little princess like that!*

Damen quickly opened the door. "Look I've got to go run out for a few minutes. I'll be back soon. I'm heading to the office."

Kimberly looked at him a bit suspicious.

"What's the rush?"

"I want all my documents prepared for tomorrow. It's Friday, I would like to leave early." He wasn't sure if she bought that one or not. "I could wait until tomorrow if you want me home." Damen started walking towards the bedroom door hoping she'd stop him, so she didn't catch him bluffing.

"Really Kimberly?" Damen asked.

"I knew you were going to the office regardless of what I said. You were just hoping I'd give you permission, in hopes that, I would feel as if I was the deciding factor on rather or not you went to the office."

"Kim, you're getting to know me too well."

"We're getting married, I should know you." Kimberly said with a smile.

"It shouldn't take long." Damen kissed her.

Kimberly gave a wave and turned back to placing the dishes into the dishwasher.

He hopped in his truck pulled out his phone and called Toya.

"Hi sexy, I was hoping you'd call."

"Are you crazy?! Why are you calling me like a stalker and making threats about coming to my house?"

"Because I need to see you."

"You don't need to see me, you want to see me. Stop it!"

"I do. You should know that your perfect little princess isn't so perfect."

"What are you talking about?"

"Your little princess has been meeting up with this guy name Josh."

"I know she had lunch with him and that she's seen him in passing at the hospital. How do you know about Josh and Kim?"

"Let's just say I have friends."

"What do your friends have to do with Kim?"

"I know that I need to see you or I will tell her about us."

"There is no us. I don't know what you're on but you need to get a hold of yourself."

"I know that Kimberly works at Northwestern Hospital on the fifth floor from 5pm to 5am. I know she drives a black Chevy Malibu. .

"What?! So now you're stalking Kimberly?"

"I'm not stalking Kimberly; I could care less about her. She's just incentive for you to do as I say. Meet me at Lexie's."

"No Toya meet me at the Starbucks across the street from your house in fifteen minutes."

"What?!"

"Yes or no deal."

"Fine."

Damen shook his head, she was crazy! Did she actually think he would meet her at Lexie's? That was Kimberly's spot. He wouldn't take another female there and risk the chance of someone telling Kimberly, that they saw him there with another woman. No way! He picked the Starbucks by her house to put some distance between her and Kimberly. If she was close to the house, she would have to turn around. Damen continued driving. He was doing about 70 mph. He made it to the Starbucks in 18 minutes, it usually took 25 minutes. He did not see her car in the parking lot. He looked down at his phone, it was Toya."

"Where are you?" Damen asked sternly.

"I'm about 5 minutes away. Don't leave." Damen was relieved to know that he still had some leverage of control over her.

"You got 3 minutes." He hung up the phone and began to time her. Damen saw Toya's car speeding into the parking lot at 2 minutes and 57 seconds. She opened the car door and started to run towards the Starbucks. He walked in after her.

"Toya"

Toya quickly turned around and followed Damen to a table. She sat across from him with a smile.

"I've missed you Damen."

"You're crazy!"

"Crazy for you."

"This is not a game."

"It could be fun."

"Listen Toya, let's get some things straight, if you ever come to my house, I'm going to shoot you, no questions asked. Secondly, I am changing my number and if you so happen to find it and call me that many times again, I am taking all those messages straight to the police so they can have their way with your crazy . . .

"Damen I understand."

"I'm not finished! Last but definitely not least, if you so much as walk past Kimberly and cause a hair strain to fall out of place, you will never work at a law firm again and I will personally terminate you". . . *Literally* Damen mouthed. Do you understand? "

Toya's eyes were dilated. "Yes."

"Now what's so important that you had to see me?"

"Damen I wanted to tell you that I . . . I am moving to New York. I wanted to be the first one to tell you. Dave said that he would talk to you tomorrow. I asked him if the new firm had any paralegals. He said no, and I asked him if I could transfer to New York. That way we can still be together."

Damen just stared at her.

"Gosh you're gorgeous." Toya said with a smile.

Okay she might be psychotic. Damen thought.

"Are you psychotic?"

"No, why are you constantly asking me if I'm crazy."

"Because if you're not, you deserve an Oscar. There's no way I'm allowing you to come New York!"

"Then I'm telling Kim about us."

"And you're fired!"

"Okay, Damen, okay. Please!" She said looking hurt.

"You are not moving to New York with Kim and I. That's not happening. And don't try to do anything crazy like filing any sexual assault charges against me. He handed her a tape. Dave's already saw this, the day after you came on to me, when you first started

104

working. I told Dave to give you a pass and that we would teach you to use your brains and not your body."

Toya stood with her mouth open.

"There are more of your little videos and texts. Any other threats or comments you would like to make?"

Toya shook her head as tears fell from eyes.

"I'm glad we were able to have this conversation and set some things straight."

Damen left the Starbucks and headed to his car.

****

When Damen arrived home he walked into the master bedroom. Kimberly was reading her bible. She smiled when she saw him.

"Hey Babe. Did you take care of things at the office?"

"I think so." Damen said with a smile as he kissed Kimberly. "I'm going to take a shower."

"Okay Babe."

Damen walked into the bathroom and quickly hopped in the shower. Once he was done he opened the door. Kimberly was asleep. He walked over to the bed and crawled in. Kimberly's phone was flashing, signaling a missed call or text. Damen picked it up. There was a missed message from Josh. It read, *Hi Kim! Do you know any tips that might help with insomnia?*

Damen responded "My Kim's sleeping, Google it."

Josh quickly replied, "I have just, thought she could give some insight, since she's a nurse."

Damen shook his head. "Should have asked her during lunch. She's only my nurse after work hour's bro." Damen placed Kimberly's phone on the nightstand and laid down.

Chapter 16

Josh

Josh pressed send and the text was sent. *He does have a point.* Josh thought, it was late to text her. He looked at Junior who was lying next to him with a book. "Still not tired Lil man?" Junior shook his head and rubbed his eyes. How about we read you one more story?"

"Yeah!" Junior crawled up next to Josh and laid his head on his chest as Josh read him another story. Junior finally fell asleep. Josh covered him and got out of bed. He walked into Mia's room she was sound asleep with her stuffed Dc. McStuffins doll. Josh gave a slight smile before heading to the kitchen. He grabbed a soda and sat down at the table. He put his head down as he held the top portion of it. He closed his eyes trying to clear his mind.

Josh looked down at the table where his mom's bible was opened and highlighted on Isaiah 40:28-31, it read,

"He giveth power to the faint; and to them that have no might he increaseth strength.

Even the youths shall faint and be weary, and the young men shall utterly fall: But they that wait upon the Lord shall renew their strength; they shall mount up with wings as eagles; they shall run, and not be weary; and they shall walk, and not faint." *Are you trying to tell me something?* Josh thought. I am tired and weary. I believed in you my whole life and where did that get me? His phone buzzed. It was a text message from Kim saying, "Huh?"

Josh responded.

"?"

"You text me an hour ago saying, *you're right, I apologize.*"

Oh! Josh remembered, he texted that message after her fiancé told him it was late and that Kimberly was only his nurse after hours. Josh didn't know why, but he felt like someone had punched him in the gut when he'd saw that text.

"Yeah, I was apologizing for texting you so late. Your fiancé didn't like that"

"Is everything okay?"

"It is."

"Don't lie, you can't sleep right?"

"You read my text."

"Really, I didn't."

"I'm good."

"I don't believe you. But when you're ready to talk about it, I'm here for you."

"I'm fine, but thanks."

"Then get some sleep. Lol goodnight."

"Goodnight."

Josh placed the phone down with a smile.

James walked into the kitchen.

"Was that Kim?"

"Yeah it was."

"She's a sweet young lady."

"She is."

James pointed to the bible on the table.

"Sneaking in a little of the word huh?"

"Nah, Mom left this."

"Oh I see? Which one of you couldn't sleep? Was it you or Junior?"

"Both" Josh said with a slight laugh.

"Do you wanna talk about it?"

"Junior's insomnia is about 4-5 X's week."

"It's gradually getting better. I'm hoping he'll grow out of it."

"Yes your Mom and I have been praying for him. We are going to go on a fast next week for both of you. You should do it with us."

"I'll pass."

"Son, how long are you going to be mad at God?"

Just then, Margaret came down stairs.

"James get back in bed, you know you are supposed to be in bed. I would have gotten whatever you needed in the kitchen. Now go on back upstairs."

James shook his head "Gotta go, the boss has spoken."

"Thank God Kim comes tomorrow." Margaret said with a smile.

Josh smiled as he watched his Mom and Dad walk up the stairs.

Chapter 17

Kimberly

Kimberly placed the juice on the table as Damen walked into the kitchen and kissed her.

"Morning Doll."

"Good morning Babe."

"I'm going out tonight with a couple of my frat brothers tonight so, I will get in late."

"That's cool, so in other words don't wait up."

"Exactly!" Damen said with a smile "What are your plans for tonight?"

"I don't know maybe go to the movies with Dee after I'm done assisting Mr. Crawley."

"Yeah the Crawleys." Damen said sarcastically.

"Damen doesn't do jealousy." Kimberly playfully responded as she pinched his cheek. Damen moved his head slightly.

Kimberly gave Damen a slight smile trying to determine if he was serious.He gave her a blank face.

"Are we serious right now?" She asked.

"Don't be so naive, he's already texting you in the middle of the night and going on lunch dates. He wants you back."

"Wow, there's that word, naive again. I don't understand why you'd get jealous if I'm so naive."

"Because I love you. Oh and let's get something straight, I'm not jealous, I'm territorial, there's a difference."

"I'm not something materialistic that you own Damen. Material things can be taken. I'm here because I want to, because I love you."

Damen looked Kim in the eyes and held her arm, "I love you too, but you are mine."

Dee came into the kitchen. "Good morning!"

"Good morning." They said in unison.

110

"What's going on? Am I interrupting . . . ? You two look serious."

"It's fine." Kim responded.

"Oh good, cause I'm starving."

****

Kimberly knocked on the door and the door immediately opened. She was greeted by Margaret.

"Hi Sweetie!" They hugged.

"Hello Mrs. Crawley."

"Come on in, James' upstairs. Josh!"

"Okay." Kimberly said with a smile.

"Josh!" Margaret called out.

"Yeah?"

"Come and help Kim with this bag please."

"Thanks but I'm fine."

"Girl let Josh help you."

Josh came into the foyer.

"Hi Kim how are you?" Josh asked as he grabbed her bag.

"I'm good."

"Granny!" Mia called

"I'm coming."Margaret responded

"I'll lead the way." Josh said with a smile.

"Yes Kimberly Josh will take you to James."

"Sound's good." Kimberly followed behind Josh.

Josh turned around, "We're acting as if you don't know your way around our house."

111

"It's been awhile."

Josh smiled "Detour, come here let me show you something."

Kimberly looked at Josh a bit bewildered.

"Remember, I'm on the job."

"I know the bosses really well, don't worry."

Josh beckoned for Kimberly. If her memory served her right, he was walking towards his bedroom. He opened the bedroom door. His room looked the same as it did when they were in high school.

"Look at this." He said holding up her class ring. "I was in here about to pack away some things and I ran across this. I never gave it back. Why didn't you ask for it?"

"At the time, that was one of the last thing on my mind." *I was heartbroken wondering why you broke things off and left.* Kimberly thought.

"Why didn't you return it?"

"Because, I wanted to keep something of yours while I was away . . . I thought about you a lot while I was gone."

"But you never thought to call or even respond to any of my letters?"

"I was coward."

"It doesn't matter."

"Yes it does, in order for us to move forward you have to be honest with me and tell me how wrong I was to leave you."

"Why, you just said it. I better get going." Kimberly walked out of the room. She stopped and said "Hi" to Junior when she saw him running towards his dad's room. Junior stopped running as he looked up at her and waved. He gave her a slight smile. "Daddy!"

"In here son."

Kimberly knocked on James bedroom door before walking in. James smiled when he saw her enter.

"How are you Mr. Crawley?"

"Like the saying goes, I'm blessed by the best."

"Yes you are." Kimberly said with a smile. "Let me start by checking your vitals, then I'll check your bandages how does that sound?"

"Sounds like I'm back at the hospital."

"But you're in the comfort of your own bed with your wife's cooking."

"You gotta point there." James said with a smile.

Kimberly smiled, "Now let's get started."

"Alright."

Once Kimberly was done assisting James she said goodbye.

"Thanks for everything Kimmie!" Margaret said. "You sure you don't want to join us for dinner? There's more than enough."

"Sounds tempting but I'm meeting my sister tonight."

"Maybe next time."

"Perhaps so."

Josh grabbed her bag. "I'll take this to the car."

"Thanks Josh. I'll see you all on Monday."

"See you Kim."

Kimberly walked outside to the car.

"Kim."

"Yes?"

". . . Thanks for helping my dad."

"Don't mention it." Kimberly smiled and got into the car.

Chapter 18

Josh

Josh watched her drive off. He wanted Kimberly in his life and more than a friend. *Sorry Lisa.* He thought. *I will tell her how I feel before she leaves for New York.* Josh walked back to the house.

****

The weekend came and went quickly, it was already Monday. Josh had a very busy week scheduled. He was going to look into purchasing two foreclosed properties as well as visit schools to select for Mia to attend in the fall. However, he made sure to keep his schedule clear for today when Kimberly came by to assist his dad. Junior finally fell asleep, after not sleeping during the night. Josh and Mia were playing memory when the doorbell rang. *That's probably Kim.* Josh looked at Mia, "Can we freeze the game for a minute? I am going to help Kim with her bag okay? "

"Ummm . . .okay daddy."

"Would you like to help?"

"No thanks."

"I'll be right back."

Josh walked to the door where his mom and Kim stood talking.

"Hi Josh" Kim said with a smile.

"Hi Kim, let me get that bag for you."

"Thank you."

Josh took the bag and noticed a scar on her right arm. He placed the bag in his parents' room. He would ask her about her arm later. Josh went back into the children's room where Mia was standing, holding a picture of Lisa. "Daddy do you still miss mommy?"

Josh was taken by surprised

"Very much so princess. I will always love and miss your mom. Do you want to talk about your mom?"

Mia nodded her head. "Would Mommy get mad if you had another woman friend?"

"No, mommy wouldn't get mad if I had another woman friend. Mommy wants you, me and Junior to be happy. When we are happy, mommy's happy and when we're sad mommy's sad. Would you get mad if I had a woman friend?"

"Ummm . . . I don't know."

"Princess no matter how many friends I have, no one can ever take you and Junior's place. I will always love you." Josh kissed Mia on the forehead.

"Love you too Daddy."

"I see your mom every time I look at you. You look and act just like your mom."

Mia smiled and gave Josh a hug.

"Let's finish the game." Josh said with a smile.

****

Josh heard Kimberly tell his mom and dad bye as she began to walk down stairs. His mom was walking down the stairs after her. Josh looked at his mom.

"I'll see her out Mom."

"Okay Sweetie." Margaret said with a smile. "I will see you Kim on Thursday."

"See you Thursday Mrs. Crawley."

Josh took Kim's bag as they walked to the foyer. Josh turned to face Kim.

"Kim, I am going to look at some properties this week. "These could be my first flips."

Josh handed her two listings for single family homes.

"Oh wow Josh! This is awesome!"

116

"I'm excited but I won't get my hopes up."

Kimberly hugged him. "I'm so happy for you." Josh smiled. I really hadn't given it much thought until you mentioned it. You see, you inspire me."

"I reminded you that's all. You were going to do it regardless." Kimberly lifted her hand to move her hair from her face and Josh saw the scar on her arm again.

Josh gently touched her arm. "What happened there?"

Kimberly pulled her arm back quickly. "I can be such a klutz; I hurt myself on a mirror."

"I've never saw you as a klutz."

"Like you said, we've changed since high school."

That was another one of her jabs at him for the past. He really wished she'd scream and yell at him, while telling him how she really felt about him ending things the way he did. He expected that. Instead she acted as if it didn't and doesn't affect her.

"Yes we have change. If I was given a second chance with you, I wouldn't leave this time."

Kimberly looked at Josh as they walked to her car. She looked surprised as she drove off. Josh walked back to the house and went inside. He could tell he surprised her when he stated he would't leave her again. How would she react when he told her how he felt? Josh had to tell her. He would not let her go this time without a fight. Kimberly's next visit would be Thursday. He would be ready.

Chapter 19

Kimberly

The nerve of Josh to tell her that! Who did he think he was, constantly making remarks like that? One minute, it seemed as if Josh was flirting with her, the next reminding her of the pain he'd caused her, as if she needed a reminder. She walked into the house and Damen's frat brother, Mark was there laughing with Dee

"Hello" Kim greeted.

"Oh hi Kim! How are you?"

"I'm good."

"I hope you don't mind, Damen said I could crash on the sofa for tonight and Friday."

"I don't mind but why tonight and Friday?"

"Because my girl comes back in town on tomorrow and I'll stay with her Tuesday through Thursday. Damen and I are going out on Friday and we won't be back until 3 or 4 in the morning. I ain't trying to hear her mouth.

Dee laughed."You see, Men ain't no good."

"Why you say that? I am preventing an argument."

"Whatever!" Dee said as she fanned her hand.

Kimberly smiled, "Yes you are welcome here Mark."

Mark walked over and hugged Kim.

"You're the best."

Damen walked in, he looked frustrated

"Hi Babe, how are you?"

"I've been better." He walked over and gave Mark a pound.

"What's up man?" Mark said with a smile.

118

"Too much man, but you know me. I'll survive." Damen walked into the bedroom.

Kimberly walked in after him. Damen looked up at her and turned his back.

"Do you want to talk about it?"

Damen didn't respond.

"Okay, I'll leave. Let me know if you want to talk about it."

"What's for dinner Kim?"

"Huh?"

"What's for dinner?"

"I was going to pick up something or maybe we could have Chinese."

"You can't cook because you're parading around, playing house with your ex right?"

"Damen I'm not doing this with you. I can see you had a bad day but don't take it out on me."

Damen stared at her.

"I don't want you working for them anymore. Tell them to find someone else."

"Damen I won't do that."

"Why not?" He pulled her arm and grabbed her closer to him.

"Damen let go of my arm, you're hurting me!" Kimberly tried to pull away.

Damen loosen his grip.

"I was willing to give up making partner for you and you can't call your ex's family to tell them you quit? Something's wrong with that."

"Damen I only have two more weeks. I gave them my word."

"So, I have no say on this matter?"

"You do, but I . . ."

"You already gave them your word." Damen interjected.

"I'm going to fix my ex's sink, don't wait up."

"Damen!" Kimberly took his arm. He pulled away. Kimberly ran in front of the door.

"Damen don't do this."

"Don't do what? I'm going to help my ex. I gave her my word as well. Now move out of the way."

"Damen."

"Kimberly please move." Kimberly moved from in front of the door. Damen stormed out of the house.

Kimberly sat down on the bed in disbelief. She closed her eyes and began to pray. *Oh God the Almighty, I am looking to you on this matter. Perhaps, Damen has a point; If Damen is right on this matter, speak to me, so that I can discontinue the services for the Crawleys. Guide me as to what to do. Strengthen Damen and I's relationship. Give us more trust and strengthen us in You. In Jesus Name. Amen.*

Kimberly opened her eyes as Dee bombarded the door.

"Girl what's up with Damen? He stormed out of the house mad!"

"We got in a fight."

"Mark left with him so there's no telling what kind of havoc they will cause."

Kimberly was silent.

"I hate seeing you down. You can tell Damen had a bad day but don't let him ruin yours."

"I won't, let's go somewhere."

"Let's go to the Sox's game." Dee suggested.

"But you don't care that much for baseball."

"It's to cheer you up. It'll be fun."

"You know I love sports. Let's get dressed!" Kimberly stated.

****

Onced at the stadium, they grabbed some hotdogs and sodas from the concession stand and immediately went to their seats.

"This should be fun." Kim said with a smile. "Thanks for suggesting this."

"No problem Sis you are always cheering me up. It's only fair that I return the favor, at least sometimes."

Kimberly smiled and responded, "Thank you."

"Hi beautiful."

Kimberly turned around. She was surprised to see Josh.

"Josh?! What are you doing here?"

"I had tickets, remember I invited you to a baseball game?"

"Oh! Yeah."

"Hi Dee how are you?" Josh asked.

"I am good, great to see you."Dee said with a big smile as she hunched Kimberly.

"This is my friend, John."

"Hi Ladies, nice to meet you." John said as he shook their hands.

"Nice meeting you as well John." "Where are your seats? Kimberly asked.

"Here 15 and 16. Where are your seats?"

"13 and 14."

"You're kidding me."

"No, no, cross my heart." Kimberly said with a smile as she playfully crossed her heart.

"It's destiny." Dee said with a raised eyebrow.

"Perhaps so." Josh said as he looked at Kimberly.

Kimberly didn't respond as she sat down. Dee deliberately sat in seat 13, so that Kimberly and Josh sat next to each other.

"I'll try not to embarrass you like I did when we dated." Kimberly said with a smile. Whenever, she attended a game she screamed a cheered loudly for her team.

Although, Josh never told her she embarrassed him, everyone else made it clear that her cheering was embarrassing.

"I never thought your cheering was embarrassing. I actually found it cute."

"Cute? Yeah sure."

"You know I don't lie Kim."

Kimberly smiled. "I haven't caught you in lie."

"I'm that good." Josh said with a smile.

"Exactly"

"Josh you're inscrutable."

Josh winked at her.

* * * *

Once the game was over they all laughed and cheered. They were excited the Sox got the win. Everyone had a good time and John fit right in.

"I'm starving!" Dee exclaimed.

"Me too" John said rubbing his stomach.

"Let's get something to eat." Dee insisted.

Josh looked at his watch, "It's getting late . . ."

"It is." Kim agreed as she looked down at her phone.

"You have no choice; remember we drove in my car." John said with a smile.

"You're right, you insisted on driving and paying for parking since I got the tickets. That's okay, there's always a cab."

"Hi Dee!" Two of Dee's good friends, Karen and Aisha were approaching them.

"Hey girls! Dee said with a smile. "This is Josh and his friend John you all know my sister, Kim."

"Nice to meet you." Josh said

"Pleasure's all ours." Aisha said with a huge grin.

"John and I wanted to grab something to eat but these two party poopers, were complaining about the time. As if they had curfews." Dee shook her head.

"Sweet! Aisha responded. "We'll join you and John."

"Then it's a deal! Kim I'll get a ride home with Karen and Aisha."

"Are you sure?"

"Yes, I'm sure. Stop worrying."

Kimberly smiled.

"Josh I can give you a ride." Kimberly stated.

John looked at Kim and smiled. "I was just joking, I got him. I would never do my boy like that."

"I figured that. Kim said "I just wanted to make sure."

"That's cool." John responded.

Josh looked at John. "John I'm gonna ride with Kim. Go get you something to eat and I'll talk to you tonight."

"You good?" John asked.

"I'm good." Josh said with a nod.

"Later man."

"Alright."

Josh followed Kim to her car.

Kimberly quickly unlocked the car doors as they climbed into the car.

Kimberly looked at her phone. Damen was calling her again this was his second time calling. She did not want to talk him right now. Damen always wanted things on his time and terms.

Kimberly saw Josh look at her phone as it vibrated.

Kimberly fasten her seat belt as she put the car in reverse before driving out of the parking lot.

"So two and half weeks before New York."

"Yes, the time is going by so fast."

The phone vibrated again.

"I know you're wondering why I'm not answering the phone."

"No."

"No?!'

"I already know why."

"Why?" Kimberly was curious.

Josh looked at Kimberly. "Do you want to talk about the problems you and Damien are having?"

"Damen his name is Damen."

"Damen." Josh repeated "Do you?"

"No. Do you want to talk to me about your insomnia?"

"I want to . . . Kimberly pull over."

"For what?"

"Just do it."

Chapter 20

Josh

Kimberly pulled the car over. Josh turned towards Kimberly. He looked at her and took her hand.

Kimberly looked abashed.

"I haven't been in Chicago for a full month and you've already encouraged and inspired me."

"Glad I could put a smile on your face." "You've put more than a smile on my face. Kim I want you back."

Kimberly pulled her hand from him and glared at him.

"I don't want you to move to New York with him. I want you to stay with me and see. . ."

"Stop it!" Kimberly said with watery eyes. "You have no right to come back here and tell me this, especially now! I loved you and you broke my heart! I waited for you, wrote you and you didn't have the decency to tell me why. I hate you for that!"

Tears started to stream down her face.

Josh wanted her to tell him how she felt about him leaving without filters. That had to happen but it hurt him to see her like this and know that he was to blame.

Kimberly opened the car door and got out of the car. Josh immediately hopped out after her. He hugged her as she cried on him.

"I'm sorry Kim, I will never hurt you like that again. I will never leave you again. I promise."

Kimberly pulled away from him.

"Kimberly please. . ."

Kimberly wiped her eyes. "Please what?"

"Kimberly I loved you and it did hurt me to leave you that way. Give me a second chance to love you the way you should be love."

Josh looked Kimberly into her eyes and kissed her.

Kimberly stepped away for him. "Don't ever do that again Josh!" She walked backed to the car.

They got back into the car. The car ride was completely silently. Neither of them said a word. Josh wanted to comfort Kim but opted not to upset her more. Once Kimberly pulled up in front of Josh's parents' house she parked the car. Josh looked at Kimberly. "Thank you for the ride."

Kimberly nodded her head as she continued looking straight ahead. Josh got out off the car and watched her as she drove off. *This was some night* he thought. Josh entered the house.

"Was that Kim's car?" Margaret asked.

"Yes Mom, she and Dee were at the game. They were seating right next to us . . . where's Junior? Is he sleep?"

"Yes."

"Oh that's great! What did you do?"

"I sang him Jesus loves me two times and he was out like a light."

"Wow!"

"I wasn't expecting you back so soon. I thought you and John were going out after the game to talk and hang out?"

"Nah, I decided to come home."

"Were you trying to hurry back to tend to Junior."

"Yes and no." Josh said with a smile.

Margaret laughed and shook her head.

"Well at least you're honest. How is my Kimmie doing? "

"She's been better."

"What do you mean?"

"She's facing some major life decisions, getting married, moving to New York."

"Seeing you again."

". . . Yeah."

"She's a sweet girl. God will comfort and lead her. The bible says *Come unto me, all ye that labour and are heavy laden, and I will give you rest.* Kimmie loves God and he loves her."

Josh smiled. *I love her too.* Josh thought.

"Well let me rest. I love you son."

"I love you too Mom. Goodnight."

"Goodnight."

Josh walked into his bedroom optimistic. He hated seeing Kimberly so upset, yet it signified she still cared for him. Why else would she get so upset?

Chapter 21

Kimberly

Kimberly pulled the visor down and looked in the mirror, her eyes were red. She sat in the car for a few minutes. *Why was she so mad?* She thought. She got out of the car and walked into the house. Damen was sitting down on the sofa. "Why didn't you answer your phone?" Damen asked.

"I didn't want to talk to you." Kimberly responded.

"That's mature."

"Well, I learned that from you."

"That's a lie. Why were you crying?"

"What?" *Nothing gets past him.* She thought. Damen's phone beeped and he looked down at his phone. "What?! What is this?" Damen exclaimed as he looked at Kimberly and then back at his phone. He quickly got up from the sofa. Damen looked infuriated as he walked towards Kimberly.

"Why are you looking at me like that?"

"I thought you were sweet and wholesome!" Damen grabbed Kimberly by the arm.

"What are you talking about?" Let me go! This wasn't enough?" Kimberly asked holding up her arm with the scar on it. That scar came from last week. Damen got upset with her, so he forcefully grabbed her arm. When she tried to pull away, he pushed her, causing her to fall on the wooden cheval mirror.

"Apparently not!" He threw her against the wall. "I thought you were different!"

"What are you talking about?!" Let me go!"

"I trusted you."

Damen grabbed Kimberly's blouse and threw her forcefully onto the bed face down, ripping her blouse.

Before Kimberly could get up Damen pushed her down again and turned her to face him."Stop it!" Kimberly screamed as she kicked him. He quickly grabbed her legs before pinning her to the bed. She wrestled and got a hand free and slapped him. Damen quickly grabbed both of her hands with his left hand and quickly slapped her twice. He lifted a fist and stared at her. "I loved you . . . but you're nothing! Nah, I never loved you. I used you! And Josh is using you too. You're too naive to see it. Kimberly kneed him and he let go of her.

Kimberly got up with tears in her eyes. *Lord please* before she could finish, Damen grabbed her arm. Kimberly pushed him hard and quickly began to walk towards the door. Damen grabbed Kimberly by her shoulders and slammed her against the door twice.

"I'm trying not to hurt you! But you're making it hard."

"What is wrong with you?"

"You're what's wrong with me."

Knock, knock.

"Yeah?!"

"Chicago Police."

Damen looked at Kim.

Damen recognized the voice and opened the door.

"Hey Jamal!" Damen and the police officer hit hands.

"Yeah man we got a call about some screams coming from your Condo everything okay?" The officer looked at Kimberly and then Damen.

"We're okay." Damen responded.

"Yeah man, you may want to keep your domestic issues a bit quieter, so the neighbors are not calling."

Kimberly grabbed her purse and quickly left the house without looking back.

Once she got inside her car she cried profusely, weeping. After tonight, Kimberly was unsure of many things. But she knew Damen and her were through. She quickly dialed Dee's number. Then texted her, "911."

Dee immediately called her.

"Hello."

"What's wrong?!"

"I'm okay, but Damen and I got into a huge argument.

Kimberly began to cry. "Dee he slapped me . . .

"What! Oh no!"

"It's like he snapped. He kept making references about Josh. I've never seen him like that before." Kimberly started to cry more. "Something's wrong."

"Yeah, he's crazy! I should go over there and . . ."

Kimberly interrupted. "Dee please leave it alone. Please. I'm hurt emotionally but I'll live. If you get involve and he puts a hand on you I will go to jail."

Dee was silent. "I'm leaving, I will be at Granny's in about ten minutes or so."

"No Dee, I'm fine. Really. I gotta call Granny. I love you and I'll talk to you later."

"I Love you too Sis."

Kimberly hung up the phone and placed her head on the steering wheel and closed her eyes. *God I need you. I know you make no mistakes, for your word says,* **Trust in the Lord with all thine heart; and lean not unto thine own understanding. In all thy**

ways acknowledge him, and shall direct thy paths. God, please direct my path. . .
and . . . Direct Damen's as well.

In Jesus's name Amen. Kimberly picked up the phone to dial her Granny, but she
thought against it. It was late, her Granny was sleeping. She would check herself and
Dee into a hotel for tonight. She would figure out the long term solution later. Kimberly
called Dee and gave her the information as well as texted her the information.

* * * *

Once at the hotel she closed the door. She quickly sat down on the bed after feeling
faint headed. The events from the day left her completely exhausted! She laid down on
the bed without pulling the covers over her.

* * * *

Kimberly rolled over and saw Dee staring at her.

"Kimmie, I couldn't sleep. I was constantly thinking about you. Damen had the nerve to
call your phone. Don't worry; I gave him an ear full."

"I know you did." Kimberly said with a pasted smile.

"He sent you this video."

Dee was looking at her like you don't want to see this.

"The way you are looking at me, do I even want to see this?"

"Yeah, you want to see this!"

Kimberly sat up, her head started pounding, and her ears began to ring a bit. She shook
her head.

"You alright?"

"Yeah. I'll be okay." Kimberly took the phone and played the video. She immediately
saw herself and Josh outside of her car. *Oh my God!* Kimberly thought. Did he have

someone following them? She watched the video of Josh kissing her and it immediately cut off. *He thinks I was cheating on him.*

"Josh kissed you last night! Oh my gosh! And Damen recorded it! Was he following us?"

"I don't know if it was him or if he had someone following us."

"I bet it was Mark!" Dee exclaimed.

Kimberly looked at Dee.

"This isn't going to be easy for me because I love him. Even after everything that transpired last night. However, we will never get back together. I am going to change my number and inform him that if he follows me, has someone else following me or if I think someone is follow me again, I will fill out a police report."

"Way to go sis!" Dee said with a smile. I've already called Granny and told her about everything."

"What?! What did you say? I told her that you and Damen got in a huge fight and that he got physical and slapped you."

"What did she say?"

"Granny started praying. Then she said, she never liked him for you and she hopes you leave him for good. I told her that we were moving in with her because I was staying with you and Damen."

"When did you talk to her?"

"About ten minutes before you woke up."

"She's probably on her way over here. Does she know where we are at?"

"Granny knows that we are at a hotel but she doesn't know the name of it, or where it is. Why? "

"Because, I don't want Granny trying to come all the way over here on the bus."

"You're right."

132

"Dee on matters such as these, I would like to be the one to tell her."

"Sure, I understand. Dee said nodding her head.

"Kim I'm going to hop in the shower."

"Alright. Dee walked into the bathroom. Kim closed her eyes. She couldn't believe Dee told their Granny before she talked to her. Ring, ring. It was Damen.

"Stop calling me!" Kimberly screamed into the phone.

"Talk to me!"

"Why should I! I never want to see you again. How could you have someone follow me?!"

"What?! I don't have anyone following you. You know that's not me."

"I don't know you Damen!"

"Yeah and I don't you know you either! Cheater!"

"Damen I've never cheated on you! That's more your style, Toya! And God only knows who else. I love you . . . loved you too much to do something like that." Kimberly eyes began to water but she would not let him know that she was crying. I guess that's what happens when you're naive! You get used right?"

". . ."

Was he still there? She thought.

"Hello?"

"Yeah, I'm still here."

"I'm changing my number and I don't want you contacting me again!" Tears continued to fall down.

Dee came out of the shower. "Hang up the phone!"

Damen responded "You don't have to do that if you want me to . . ." Dee snatched the phone.

"Stop calling my sister! If you keep stalking her we are getting the police involved!"

Click.

"Kimberly what are you doing?! Why are you talking to him?!"

"I told you I would talk to him about having people following me around! I told you that Dee!"

"I don't think you need to talk to him if you're going to get this emotional."

"It's my job to stand up to Damen and to tell him how I feel. I'm going to take a shower."

Kimberly looked at Dee. "And Dee . . . I appreciate you looking out for me, I do. I'm going to cry sometimes because I'm emotional but I'll be okay. Okay?"

"I'm your sister and I will always look after you. That's what sisters do."

"I know." Kimberly said with a smile.

Chapter 22

Damen

Knock, knock. Damen quickly opened the door. Mark quickly came in.

"What's going on? I got your message."

"Mark man, I really messed up."

"What do you mean?"

"I was having a crazy day yesterday. I was informed by a friend that my Dad's been looking for me, my Mom and Cam." Damen shook his head. "That's why I was upset when I arrived home yesterday. Then to make matters worse, look at this video." Damen handed Mark the phone.

"What?!" Mark looked up at Damen. "Who is this dude?"

"That's Kimberly's ex, Josh."

"That's so not like Kim to cheat on you man." Mark shook his head. "Let's not jump into conclusion. He clearly kissed her, she didn't kiss him back." Mark rewind the video. "What did she say?"

"I didn't give her a chance to say anything. . . I grabbed and slapped her."

"Wow! Wait . . .What?! Where is she?" Mark looked towards their bedroom door.

"She's not there. I overreacted man."

Mark walked over to Damen and placed his hand on his shoulder. "Kim's a good woman. She loves you a lot. Perhaps with time she'll forgive you."

"Nah, she's gone man." *Mark's not even her fiancé and he gave Kim the benefit of doubt.* He thought. *Why hadn't he?*

"How did you get this video?"

"A friend of mine texted it to me. He said Toya text him this asking if that was my girl."

"Toya?!"

"She and the friend went to school together."

"Wow, it's a small world. . . Look Damen, I can try to talk to Kim."

"No thanks."

"Player Damen isn't trying to make a comeback is he?"

Damen smiled.

"I liked Kim, she was good for you."

"Apparently, the truth is, I'm not good for her. It hurts man because I actually loved this one. I was hurt man. I thought she'd cheated on me. So, I tried to hurt her physically and emotionally. Kimberly told me how Josh left her and how it took her some time to get over the heartbreak. So I even brought that up to hurt her more."

"What?! Mark questioned.

Damen knew what it was; he'd fallen in love and for the first time and had his heart broken.

"This is crazy." Damen stated. "I've apologized to her and vented to you. It's time to move on. Thanks for listening man."

Mark stared at him. "You're hurt, you loved her."

"I am and I do, but I'm not going to lose sleep over something I can't change."

Mark continued to stare at Damen. Man we've all been here before some of us several times. This is your first heartbreak. I'm here for. Do you wanna get out of here and have some fun?"

"Let's do it!" Damen said with a smile. He and Mark partied all night long.

* * * *

It had been a week since the fight. Damen looked down at his watch. He would go home for lunch again since it was Kim's day off. He wanted to see if she would come to their place to pick up her things. He grabbed his briefcase and walked out of his office.

"Heather let Dave know I'm going to lunch."

"Sure Mr. Moore."

Once in the parking lot, Damen climbed into his truck and headed to their place. When he arrived, Damen smiled when he saw her car outside. *Thank God* He thought. He couldn't deny that he missed her. Damen was actually excited to see her. He had no idea as to what he would say to her, he just wanted to see her. Damen slowly unlocked the door and opened it slowly. Kimberly swiftly turned around. She looked beautiful. She had this glow about her.

"Gosh you're beautiful." Damen said with a devious smile. Kimberly looked as if she had saw a ghost.

"What are you doing here?!"

"Uhh . . . I live here." Damen said with a smile.

Kimberly quickly began to walk towards their master bedroom. Damen stood in front of her. Doll, I just wanted to see you and tell you that I'm sorry."

"Okay, you said it."

"Don't be that way."

She looked nervous as she looked towards the bathroom.

"What way would you like for me to be? You slapped me twice, slammed me against the wall and pinned me to the bed."

Damen nodded his head. "I was wrong. I'm wrong for you. I know that but It doesn't erase the fact that I love you. I still want you. I've never told you this, but my dad was abusive to me and my mom and. . ."

Kimberly placed her hand up to her mouth and ran into the bathroom. Damen followed her into the bathroom.

Kimberly began vomiting into the toilet. Damen looked on the sink and it was a pregnancy test. *No way!* Damen thought. He quickly walked over and picked up the test.

+

Damen was speechless. He looked at Kim as she wiped her mouth. Her eyes were dilated, "What does it say?!"

"You're pregnant."

"What?!" Kimberly snatched the test.

"No!" She began to cry. Damen just stared at her without saying a word.

"God?!" Kimberly screamed.

Damen was completely stunned. He wasn't ready to be a dad. He feared turning into his dad. But he loved Kim and the fetus already.

"Kim it's going to be okay."

Kimberly looked at him. "I never wanted to see or talk to you again! Now. . .now . . ."

"We'll keep in touch for the sake of our baby." Damen stated.

Kimberly was silent. She looked at Damen. "You just told me that your dad was abusive, you're abusive..."

"I've been abusive. I can go and get help with that Doll. I am going be a good dad. You'll see."

Kimberly got up and wiped her eyes.

"I've got to go." Kimberly said as she stood up.

"Can I get your number? I mean since you're pregnant with my kid."

"I will be in touch with you Damen."

Damen nodded his head and watched her as she left the apartment. *God, I'm going to be a dad.* Damen thought.

"Wow!"

Chapter 23

Kimberly

Kimberly picked up the phone and dialed Dee.

"Hello."

"Dee I'm pregnant."

"What?! Oh my gosh! Have you told Granny?"

"Not yet."

"Does Damen know?"

"Yes."

"What did he say?"

"He didn't say much but he tried to be supportive."

"Oh wow! Now he's forever, a part of your life . . . our lives."

". . ."

"Kim, I'm sorry. It's going to be alright."

". . . I've got to get going."

"That's right you're going to the Crawley's. I will talk to you later." "Alright Dee."

Kimberly hung up the phone before starting the car.

* * * *

Kimberly rang the doorbell. Josh opened the door. "Hi how are you?" Josh asked.

"I've been better."

"You want to talk about it?"

"Not really."

Josh looked at her.

"Have you been crying?

"I'm okay Josh." Josh grabbed her bag and carried it into the house.

"It will get better."

"Huh?"

"Dee called me and told me that you and Damen were done because of this big fight you had last week."

"Sometimes Dee talks too much."

"I hated when Lisa and I got into fights. It would mess up my whole night."

Kimberly smiled.

Josh started to laugh.

Kimberly looked at him bewildered.

"Remember we promised to never go to sleep angry after reading Ephesians 4:26 where it says, *"Be ye angry, and sin not: let the not the sun go down upon your wrath:"*

We would call each other at 11:58 and 11:59 to apologize."

Kimberly laughed out loud. "Yeah that was funny. We were so silly." She looked at Josh and smiled. "Where's your Mom and the kids?"

"You're going to kill me!"

"Why?"

"I volunteered to call you. I was supposed to tell you that they were taking the kids to zoo today."

"Mr. Crawley knows . . ."

"He's doing well." Josh interrupted. "It's almost been a month. He's moving around, he's not in any pain and he's still cancer free. Thank God!"

Kimberly looked at Josh confusingly. "Thank God?"

"Yeah, some of the things that's been happening lately has sort of renewed my faith."

"That's great! You're dad being healed from cancer is enough to renew one's faith alone but you said things. So what else?"

"I've purchased my first two properties to flip of which, I've started flipping.

It's going well . . . and you."

Kimberly looked up at him.

"Josh . . ."

"Kim you inspire me, you make me feel as if I can accomplish all of my dreams. I haven't felt this way since pre diagnosis of post traumatic stress."

"I didn't know you suffered from that."

"Yeah, I do. Some nights, I can't sleep. I have flashbacks of events that took place during those tours. Sometimes when I close my eyes, I see the horrific scenes of my friends lying dead beside me. I question myself if I had did this, moved faster could I have saved some lives." Josh looked at Kimberly. "I'm telling you this because when we get together this time, I want you to know exactly what you're facing. My kids mean the world to me. So I put their needs before mine, yet I will never neglect your needs and wants . . ."

"Josh!" Kimberly interrupted.

"I'm not interested in being in a relationship. I just want and need to be single for awhile."

"I understand, you just got out of a relationship. For now, all I'm asking is to be your friend in hopes of being your beau."

"I'm pregnant."

Josh looked surprised.

"Since we're putting everything on the table."

". . . I still love you Kim."

"You don't love me. I'm pregnant and confused. I have feelings for you but I'm still in love with Damen. I can't be with him because he's abusive and . . ."

"Abusive?!" He's put his hands on you?!"

Why did I let that slip out? Kimberly thought. She could tell Josh was enraged.

"It's over between him and I because of that."

Josh stared at her. "I have no respect for a man that puts his hands on a woman."

"I'm okay. Really! . . . I'd love to see your fixer upper."

Josh continued to stare at her before giving her a smile. "Let's go." Josh grabbed her bag and placed it in her car. Kimberly walked to his car. Josh opened her door before getting in.

"How did Ms. Sadie take it when you told her you were pregnant?"

"I haven't told her yet."

"What?!"

"I just found out today."

"So that explains why you were crying."

Kimberly nodded her head. "Tell me about this fixer upper."

"It's a single family, 3beds, 2bath home. 1200 square feet brick bungalow. The basement is unfinished and requires some work but I'm excited."

"I'm happy for you."

Chapter 24

Josh

"Here we are." Kimberly got out the car with a smile. "This is nice!"

Josh tossed her the keys. "Check it out." Kimberly caught the keys and opened the door. Josh followed behind her. Kimberly extended her arms, "I like that the living and dining rooms are opened. It allows lots of natural light to come inside." Josh took her hand, "Look at this kitchen."

"This is massive! Oh my goodness."

"I'm going to leave the cabinets. I'll just paint them and add new handles." Josh touched the counter tops."I am going to replace these with granite. I will add stainless steel appliances such as the refrigerator, stove and dishwasher."

"Wow! This is awesome Josh."

Josh smiled. "You like it?"

"I love it."

"Let me show you the spacious bedrooms." Josh opened the first door, "This will probably Mia's room. I think she'll pick it because it's the second biggest." They walked into another room. "This is where Junior will keep his stuff."

"Keep his stuff? Where would he sleep?"

"Junior sleeps with me." Josh looked at Kimberly. She nodded her head.

"Come this is going to be the master bedroom. I am going to knock this wall out to add more space for a nice master bathroom. Currently the attic is the master bedroom, it will be my parents' room and serve as a guest room when they're not here." Kimberly smiled. Josh smiled at her.

"The basement needs a lot of work. Since you're pregnant, I will show you the before and after pics."

"Is there mold down there?"

"No."

"Then I'm going down. I'm pregnant, not helpless."

Josh shook his head. "Be careful Kim."

"I will." She responded.

They went to the basement and looked around. After they were done they walked back to the car.

"I'm starving."Josh said. "I think the baby's hungry too."

"I am hungry." Kimberly responded. "Let's google some restaurants nearby."

Josh quickly glanced over at Kim. She was browsing on her phone for local restaurants.

"I wanna try this place it's a little farther west called McArthur's. Do you wanna try it?"

"I've ate there before, the food is delicious! Let's go."

They arrived at McArthur's ordered their food and sat down.

Josh observed her as she held her head down and prayed over her food.

Kimberly looked at him with a smile, "It's time to dig in." She began to eat.

Josh pulled out his phone, "You have this to look forward to. No matter where you are, you want to check in on your kids. I know they're in good hands but it's a parent thing."

Kimberly smiled.

"Hi Mom, how's everything?"

"Everything's going well. Junior's really having a blast."

"He's never been to the zoo before. Mia has been several times."

"Oh then that explains it. He's staring at each animal for an extended amount of time. Mia's laughing and excited to see the . . .

"Monkeys" Josh responded.

"Exactly!" Margaret laughed.

"She loves them'."

"Would you like to talk to them?"

"No thanks. They're having a good time. How is Dad?

"He's doing great! He's keeping up with the kids better than I am."

Josh laughed. "That's Dad. I'll see you guys when you come home. Love you Mom."

"Love you too son."

Josh hung up the phone.

"How's your food Kim?"

"Umm . . . it's good."

Josh started to taste his yams.

"I love this dressing and graving." Kimberly stated.

"Really, I was torn between the dressing and yams."

"Would you like to try some?"

"Sure."

"Good cause I want to try some of your yams." Kimberly quickly sampled the yams.

Josh stared at her.

Kim covered her mouth and laughed out loud. "What?!"

"Nothing" He said with a smile.

"Then eat your food." Kimberly said playfully.

They laughed, talked and lost track of time. Kimberly looked down at her watch. "Oh my goodness! I've got to go. I promised Dee I would pick her up. I have less than thirty minutes to get her."

"I can take you to get her and drop you back off to get your car."

"Thanks." Kimberly picked up her phone and called Dee.

"Hi Dee we are on our way. We should be there in about fifteen minutes."

"Who is we?"

"Josh"

"Josh?!"

"No, it's not like that."

"I'll see you in a few minutes." Kimberly hung up the phone.

"I like Dee, she's funny."

"She is. She likes you too Josh."

* * * *

Dee immediately came outside of the hotel with a smile.

"Hi Josh."

"Hi Dee, how are you?"

"Good, good."

"Awesome, we are going to get Kim's car now."

"Yeah where's Kim car?"

"You won't believe it. Tell her Josh."

"It's at my fixer upper."

"Oh nice."

"It's very nice. He has great ideas for the home."

"Can't wait to see the finishing touches." Dee stated.

"Absolutely, I will throw an open house, party and you two are invited." Josh said with a smile.

They continued talking until they arrived at the fixer upper. Josh dropped them off in front of Kimberly's car. He got out and opened the doors for them.

"Thanks Josh."

"Don't mention it."

"I want to thank you." Kimberly replied. "You turned what I considered a challenging day into a great one. I appreciate it"

"Come here." Josh extended his arm and gave her a hug."You're welcome. "

He said as he kissed her on the forehead."

"See you later Kim."

"Bye Josh."

Josh watched as they drove off.

He called his mom.

"Hi honey, where are you?"

"I am at the fixer upper on Franklin. I am going to make a stop. I should be home in about forty- five minutes."

"Okay Josh."

"Love you Mom."

"Love you too."

Josh hung up the phone. *It about time I pay Damen a visit.* He thought. Josh parked the car and entered into the complex. Luckily, someone was leaving the building. Josh was able to enter without being buzzed in. Josh hopped on the elevator to the top the floor. He got off on the 5th floor and headed to 5A. He knocked on the door. "Yeah?" Damen responded as he opened the door. He must have recognized him because he frowned when he saw him. Josh immediately punched Damen in the face. "Don't you ever put your hands on Kim again!" Damen quickly grabbed Josh and threw him into the wall. He swung at Josh. Josh ducked and punched him in the stomach before someone was standing in the middle of them. "You've better leave; the cops have already been called." The guy said."No Mark let him stay." Damen said with a smile. "I was wondering when you'd man up and talk to me. You've wanted Kim since you've came back but she's mine. Did she tell you that she's pregnant with my kid?" Josh ignored him. Damen continued, "You weren't man enough to keep her, you for sure ain't man enough to take her."

Josh walked towards Damen and Mark stood in front of Josh. "If you put your hands on her again, it will take more than your friend and the cops to get me off of you." Josh started to walk away.

"Hey, if you come back to my place again you will be greeted with a bullet."

Josh turned around and stared at him. "I'm not afraid of bullets."

Damen smiled, "You've been warned."

Josh walked out of the building and hopped in his car. He disliked Damen, he truly enjoyed punching him.

* * * *

"Daddy!" Junior said as Josh closed the door. "We saw many, many animals!"

"Yeah, which one's your favorite?"

"The lions! Rrwwww!"

"You like the roaring lions huh?"

Junior smiled and nodded his head.

"Daddy! Look what I got!" Mia was holding a stuffed monkey.

"I like it. Who got that for you?"

"Papa!"

"That was nice of him. Did you tell him thank you?"

"Like a thousand times. I told him he was the second bestest."

"Oh really." Josh said as he lifted Mia and started to tickle her. Mia laughed out loud.

"I got this one Daddy but I don't want the tickles."

Josh looked down at Junior holding a stuffed lion. He took the stuffed lion.

"You don't want the tickles?"

"No."

"Then how about a pound."

Junior smiled and nodded his head.

Josh gave him a pound.

"Did Papa get this for you too?"

"Um hmm." Junior said nodding his head with a smile.

"Nice."

Josh turned around and saw his parents smiling at them. "We had a blast son." James said with a laugh.

"I can tell." Josh responded.

Chapter 25

Kimberly

Kimberly and Dee walked into the house.

"Hi Girls."

"Hello Granny, I need to talk to you."

"Oh dear, what's wrong?"

". . ."

"Kimmie?"

"I'm pregnant.

"Pregnant?! Kimmie! . . . "

"I'm sorry."

"You and Damen have to make this work now. It's not just about the two of you, y'all have to think about what's best for this baby."

"Damen and I will do what's best for the baby. Really."

"God have mercy!" Sadie shook her head and looked Kimberly up and down. "I love you Kimmie and I will support you and this baby any way I can."

"Thanks Granny. I love you too."

"Our family will be okay because a family that prays together. . ."

"Stays together." They said in unison.

"Come and give me a hug." Sadie said with a smile as Kimberly hugged her.

"You too Dee." Dee smiled as they gave each other a group hug.

* * * *

Five Months Later

Kimberly smiled as she left her patient's room. She went to the nurses' station. "Sharon I am going to lunch. She rubbed her belly I, think she's ready to eat. I am craving some barbecue."

"That sounds good."

"Would you like for me to bring you some back?" Kimberly asked.

"Would you?"

"Sure."

"I will go to lunch when you and baby come back. Remember it's time to start thinking about names."

"I will soon. I am just wondering how her little face will look. Will she look like me or more like her dad?" She said with a smile.

"She's lucky because both her parents are beautiful."

"Awww thanks Sharon."

"It's the truth, your baby's going to be beautiful and spoiled."

"Damen's already got her some designer dresses. Not me. I am not buying her hundred dollar dresses to puke on. I don't think so."

"You haven't bought her anything right?"

"I'm waiting until I'm at least six months and a half."

"I'm gonna wait too, but then I am going to go crazy." Kimberly laughed.

"I know you will Miss. Fashionista."

Sharon laughed. I'm gonna take lunch with you. "Macy Kim and I are taking lunch together. All of our patients have been taken care of and should be fine until we get back if they need anything extra, can you and Maria take care of them?"

"Sure, no problem."

"Thanks Macy." Kimberly said.

Macy got up from the nurses' station and rubbed Kimberly's stomach."Yeah go feed our baby girl."

Kimberly and Sharon grabbed their things and headed to the parking lot.

"Damen came here yesterday with lunch for you, he forgot it was your day off."

"What?! He didn't mention it."

"You've got two great guys to choose from and I don't even have one."

Kimberly shook her head as she drove out of the parking lot.

"I don't have one." Kimberly responded.

"But by choice. If I had to choose one, it would probably be Josh. He is fine. He's so in love with you and such a manly man. He looks like he's ready to settle down. I mean he's already been married and has kids. He's ready. Then there's Damen! Oh my, he's gorgeous, successful and fun. He loves you too, I mean he passed up making partner in New York for you."

"For the baby but they made him partner in Chicago."

"Yeah, yeah, Damen loves you too but he doesn't want to get hurt. He's that type."

"Sharon I care for them. But I've been hurt by them as well. I thinks it's better for all of us if we keep our relationship platonic. My relationship with God is at an all time high. I am looking to him for all of my wants and needs."

"That's good you're building your relationship with God. Let's take the streets Kim, I don't like the expressway. I know I'm the passenger but those cars going so fast makes me nervous though."

"Okay."

Sharon turned on the radio and Tamela Mann's I can only imagine was playing. "This is nice but, I have to hear somebody moving music."

Kimberly laughed.

Sharon stopped the radio on Beyonce's and Nicki's flawless and started dancing and singing, "I'm feelin' myself, I'm feelin myself." Sharon looked over at Kimberly. She was smiling as Sharon song along.

"Oh my God!" Kimberly screamed

"What's wrong?"

"The breaks!"

"Kim watch out!"

* * * *

Damen walked out of the courtroom with a big smile. Another win that always felt good. He pulled out his phone after hearing it vibrate inside his brief case. He looked at his phone it read Dee. Damen frown a bit, Dee never called him. "Hi Dee what's up?"

"Damen Kim's been in a really bad car accident! They're doing an emergency c section to save the baby. Damen they're saying she might not make it!"

Damen froze. "What! What hospital?"

"Northwestern Hospital where she works. They're going to do all they can and then some for her."

"I'm on my way! Dave! I've gotta go!"

Damen ran to the parking lot without stopping.

He picked up his phone and called his mom.

"Hey Honey!"

"Mom Kim's been in a bad accident, they're doing an emergency c- section for the baby."

"What?!"

"They're at Northwestern, they don't know if she's going to make it!"

"Oh God no! I am on my way now."

Damen didn't stop at stop signs, he wanted to run lights. Once on the expressway, he drove way over the speed limit. *God, I know I've been playing around and only going to church and reading the Bible when it benefited me. Please God have mercy on me don't take my daughter. Please, please* spare her life and Kim's. God, I love her. Please don't take her away from me, away from all those who love her. In Jesus name. Amen. When he arrived inside the hospital, Damen ran to the desk, "Oh my God Damen! She's in intensive care!" The woman began to cry as she told him the room. Damen ran to the elevator and immediately got on. He got off and saw Dee crying. Sadie was walking back and forth praying. Dee looked up at Damen. "They're not letting us in right now! She's still in surgery."

Damen hugged Dee. "It's going to be alright." Damen didn't know that. He just had to tell Dee and himself that until he believed it. Dee continued to cry as she sat down on the sofa. Damen walked over and looked outside the window. He couldn't remember the last time he felt so helpless. The doctor came out, everyone turned to him. We were able to remove the baby she's very weak but she's a fighter. She's only three pounds and she's not in the clear yet."

"Can we see her?" Damen quickly asked.

"Yes, really soon, but no one can hold her yet. We will come and get you when viewing is permitted.

"How about my Kimmie?" Sadie asked.

"We are prepping her for another emergency surgery. We are going to do all we can."

"How's Sharon?" Dee asked. "We know she was in the car too."

"She stable."

"Thank God!" Sadie said with a sigh of relief.

Damen's mom, Karla walked off the elevator with tears in her eyes. "Damen my sweet boy!" She walked over to him and hugged him. "What are they saying?"

"Kim is not doing well they're prepping her for another emergency surgery."

"No!"

"We are going to be able to see the baby once they've got her stable. She's only three pounds Mom. The doctor said she's very weak." Damen looked at his mom with tears in his eyes. "Mom, I can't lose my daughter. I haven't even gotten the chance to get to know her." He lowered his voice and looked at his mom. "I can't lose Kim either Mom. I love her." He held his head down and cried. Karla held him tight. She hated to see her son in so much pain. Karla couldn't remembered the last time he cried. She just remembered he was a little boy. *I've got to pull myself together.* Damen thought. He wiped his eyes and lifted his head. Just then Cam arrived with Josh, James, Margaret and Josh's children. Margaret and Sadie immediately hugged.

"Sadie! How is Kim? We came as soon as we got your message." Margaret said.

"The doctors are doing all they can for her. She's already undergone two surgeries." Dee started crying again. Josh walked over to her and gave her a hug. He was silent as he hugged her.

Damen looked at him before looking at his Sister, Cam. Cam came over and gave him a hug.

"Mom filled me in about the baby. She's your daughter Damen so she's a fighter, she's part Kim so she's determined. We've got a determined, fighter. She's going to be okay."

Damen looked at her, "I sure hope so Sis. I can't lose my little girl."

"You won't Damen."

Damen walked up to the nurses' station, "How much longer before we hear anything about Kim and or the baby."

"Damen as soon as we hear something we will let you all know."

"This is frustrating! Can you give me an estimate?! That's my girl and my baby dying and you . . ."

Karla took Damen by the arm. "Come on Sweetie, let's, let them do their job. Damen shook his head.

Chapter 26

Josh

Josh looked at everyone before he started to speak. He knew God was not going to

take Kim. He just felt this still small voice saying *everything will work out.* "Listen

everyone." Josh started, "We need God to perform a miracle. The bible says, **for where**

two or three are gathered together in my name, there I am in the mist of them.

Let's bring him in the mist of us as we pray for Kim and the baby."

"Let's do it!" Dee said as she grabbed Josh's hand. Margaret, Sadie and James

followed. Karla walked over, then Damen and Cam.

Josh looked at his two children. Mia immediately ran over and grabbed his hand. "Junior

come and be a part of our prayer circle." Junior came over and took Mia's hand. *God*

The Almighty, we come to thee in need of a miraculous healing. Please touch Kim and

the baby's bodies. Strengthen and heal them from the crowns of their heads to the soles

of their feet. Go into the operating room and guide the doctor's hands as they assist with

these miracles. We know that you can do all things but fail. Your word says, The power

of life and death lies in the tongue. God we are speaking life! Life for Kim and life for the

baby. In Jesus' mighty name we pray. Amen."

"Amen!" They all said in unison.

Sadie looked at Josh, "That was beautiful, thank you for that word of prayer."

"You're welcome Miss. Sadie."

Josh looked over at Damen who was silently sitting next to his mom and sister. He

seemed calmer after the prayer. The doctor came out and everyone stared at him as

they stood up. "The baby is currently stable."

"Thank God! Karla screamed.

158

"What about Kim?" Sadie asked.

"The doctors are still working with her. She needed a blood transfusion, she lost a lot of blood. We had to remove her spleen and are preparing to move her to the ICU."

"Why is it taking so long?!"Dee asked. "I just need to know my sister will be okay."

The doctor looked at Dee. "Kim's fighting for her life and we're going to do all we can to help her."

Sadie hugged Dee as she wiped a tear from her eye.

The doctor looked at Damen. "If it's okay with Dad, we are going to let you all see her. Only He can come into her room though."

Damen looked up at the doctor.

"Can I see her now?" Damen asked.

"Yes."

Chapter 27

Damen

Damen's heart was pounding. He looked at his mom, "I'm nervous and anxious at the same time. I feel guilty seeing her without Kim."

"Kim will see her soon. We are all excited to see her. Damen lifted his eyebrows and followed the doctor as he explained to him, his daughter's condition. He warned him that she had several tubes connected to her, one of which was to assist her with her breathing.

The doctor introduced Damen to nurse before leaving. Damen walked in with the nurse after putting on his protective gear. He walked over to the glass and peered in. She was beautiful. Yes, she was very tiny and connected to a few tubes but she was perfect. Damen knew he would never be the same again.

"You can touch her." The nurse said with a smile.

Damen smiled, the first time in hours."Hi beautiful, this is your Dad. You've stolen my heart in less than 10 seconds." He looked at her and smiled. "You've got some folks anxious to meet you." The nurse pulled the curtain to the window and everyone was, "Oohing and awwing." His mom and Miss. Sadie were crying.

Damen looked at his daughter, "You're going to melt your mother's heart. You've already got Daddy wrapped around your fingers."

The nurse smiled."She's beautiful."

"Thank you. How long will she be connected to these tubes?"

"Just until she's able to breathe a little better on her own. She's a fighter, so I'll say soon.

Damen stared down at her again; amazed that someone so small could have such a big impact in his life. From now on she was his top priority. After visiting her he came back out to the waiting room. Josh was still there even though his family was gone. It didn't surprise Damen, he knew why he was there. Karla looked at Damen "She's beautiful!"

"Yes she is Bro." Cam said with smile.

"We can't wait to hold her!" Dee said with a smile.

"Kimmie's going to love her!" Sadie beamed.

Just then the doctor came out, "The surgeries were successful. However, she is in a coma."

"Then how were the surgeries successfully?" Dee asked.

"In that, we were able to stabilize her. We will make an exception and allow two people to stay overnight with her.

I know Damen and is it going to be you Miss Sadie right?" The doctor asked.

"Absolutely I will be here every night."

"Okay, they've already set up the room."

Damen looked at Miss. Sadie, "Can I stay with her tonight?"

"No, I'm staying with my sister tonight!" Dee replied.

Miss. Sadie looked at Damen. "Maybe tomorrow."

Damen wasn't going to leave without a fight.

Damen walked over to the doctor.

"Kim's grandma and Sister want to stay in the room with her. Since we're not married yet, technically Miss Sadie has the last words. However, I can't leave her tonight. Can I just sleep in the waiting area? I want to be here in case she wakes up."

The doctor looked at him, "I'll squeeze a recliner in the room for you tonight, but only tonight."

"That's fine, thanks."

Josh looked at Dee. "Dee keep me informed about everything big or small."

"I will Josh." Dee responded.

"Can I see Kim before I leave?" Josh asked the doctor.

"Briefly."

They all went into Kim's room. Josh walked over to her bed and kissed her forehead. "Hi Beautiful it's me, Josh. You gave us all a scare tonight . . . but we know who to look to, in time of troubles and triumphs. Come back to us . . . to me. . ."

"Damen cleared his throat. *Are you really going to do this here?* Damen thought. Josh looked at him and continued.

"Kim, our lives are not complete without you. We're waiting on you. I love you." Josh kissed her hand before leaving. "I'll see you all tomorrow."

"Bye Josh" Dee said.

"See you tomorrow Josh, keep praying for her. God is going to bring her back to us." Sadie said with a slight smile.

"I know." Josh said matter of factly.

"Call me if anything happens Goodnight."

"Goodnight." Dee and Sadie said together.

Sadie walked over and kissed Kim on the cheek. "You've been through a lot today, so I'll let you rest tonight but I need you to wake up tomorrow you hear me? I'm not going to lose you."

Dee chimed in "Yes, you gotta wake up. I need my big Sister. Who else will bail me out when I get in trouble? I love you Kimmie."

Damen watched and listened as they spoke to Kim.

They all prepared for bed. Sadie prayed several times before she laid down.

Dee was the first to fall asleep then Sadie. Damen moved his chair on the side of Sadie so that he was sitting next to her. "Hi Sleeping Beauty, this is me, Damen . .. You've got me doing things I don't usually do. He looked around at Dee and Sadie, making sure they were sleep. "God it's me again, Damen. I know everyone's praying for her . . . but I figured. . . Ummm . . . it couldn't hurt if I prayed too. I know I don't pray . . . but can she stay with us. Heaven has some angels.Can we keep this one?" He held his head down as he felt a tear coming down. He wiped his eyes and took her hand. "Look Doll, I need you to wake up. We've got a beautiful little baby girl. She's a fighter, but she needs her mother. I have accepted the fact that we won't be together, but I don't want to lose you entirely. Kim wake up so you can meet our daughter, she's perfect just like you. . .

Kimberly moved her eyes.

"Kim?!"

Damen felt Kimberly's hand move inside his.

God please! Damen thought.

"Nurse!"